VIRAGO
MODERN CLASSICS
482

*R. M. Dashwood*

Rosamund Dashwood was born in 1924 in a small village deep in the Devonshire countryside. Her mother, E. M. Delafield, was the celebrated author of *The Diary of a Provincial Lady*, and her father, Col. A. P. Dashwood, O.B.E., was an engineer who had built the massive docks at Hong Kong Harbour.

During World War Two, Rosamund joined the WAAF, eventually becoming a sergeant and working with the newly invented and top secret RADAR. After the war, she attended Somerville College, where she met her future husband, Leslie Truelove, introduced to her as 'the nastiest man in Oxford'.

After living in England, New Zealand and Scotland, the couple settled in Vancouver, Canada with their four sons. Rosamund has discovered a talent and consuming passion for distance running. She has completed several marathons and is the holder of four gold medals from the World Seniors' Games in Oregon, USA. She continues to write, most recently for *The Oldie*.

# PROVINCIAL DAUGHTER

R. M. Dashwood

ILLUSTRATED BY
*Gordon Davies*

Virago

A *Virago* Book

Published by Virago Press 2002
Reprinted 2004

First published in Great Britain
by Chatto & Windus Ltd 1961

A CIP catalogue record for this book
is available from the British Library.

ISBN 1 86049 950 3

Typeset in Bembo by M Rules
Printed and bound in Great Britain
by Clays Ltd, St Ives plc

Virago
An imprint of
Time Warner Book Group UK
Brettenham House
Lancaster Place
London WC2E 7EN

www.virago.co.uk

For
Paul, Simon and Patrick

# Note

It was in the 'thirties that my mother, E. M. Delafield, wrote *The Diary of a Provincial Lady* and its sequels, as a light-hearted picture of domestic life in England at that time.

This book is intended as an equally light-hearted continuation of that picture; the Provincial Lady's daughter in the 'fifties. It seemed natural to write it in the same idiom; but if the result seems to any reader too imitative, or even plagiaristic, I can only ask their forgiveness, as the original Provincial Lady would, I am sure, most warmly have given hers.

R. M. DASHWOOD

# PROVINCIAL
# DAUGHTER

# SEPTEMBER

*Monday, 10th*

Am disconcerted, at breakfast, to receive letter from old school friend saying What am I doing with My Brain these days, and isn't it a Pity to Let It All Go? Know what she means but am very angry nevertheless, and lose myself thinking out some really telling replies.

Am recalled by Toby asking thoughtfully How Do You Make Soggy Paper? and by Ben flinging toast in all directions from his high chair. Two older children applaud this warmly, and James says, in tones of utmost besottedness, that Ben's Manners are *Atrociable*. Lift Ben down and send all three children away and give Lee a second cup of tea— (why can't men help themselves?).

Return to letter from old school friend and ponder deeply; am I wasting whatever brain I had and a very expensive education? Resolve to keep meticulous record of activities for a while and *see*. Ask Lee if he thinks I should keep a diary? He replies that he thinks the blasted boiler has gone out and do I know if James borrowed his chopper because he can't find it and What did I Say? Make up my own mind to ask for no further advice but to keep diary. *Later.* Achieve washing, incredible number of shirts, shorts and underpants, all in the last stages of grubbiness. Normally efficient small washing machine obviously finds it all too much and thick grey water cascades over floor.

(New linoleum. When the men laid it they warned me never to get it wet.) Mop laboriously with retired nappy. James and Toby join in enthusiastically with nappies that I later discover not to be retired at all but straight from the Airing Cupboard. Ben saunters in and with obvious memories of recent summer holiday at seaside, dabbles and splashes joyfully. Send them all away angrily. (Good mothers never lose their tempers. I am not a good mother.) Finally finish mopping floor, hang out washing in rain, and hurry upstairs to make beds.

Had forgotten that due to Ben's recent climbing excesses

Lee has stopped up every conceivable danger point with home-made gates—(dismembered play-pen). Progress upstairs, laden with Vacuum Cleaner, mop, duster, etc., resembles Gymkhana Event. Over the gate . . . the in-and-out . . . the stile . . . and, oh dear, the Water-jump. Oh Ben!

Deposit cleaning materials, retrace laborious progress, find Ben ("Ooh, Mummie, he's *sopping*"), cart him over Gymkhana Course and change him. James and Toby join us and offer to Do the Vacuuming. They fight bitterly as to who shall be first to exercise this great privilege. My suggestion that they might make their own beds too is apparently inaudible. Make beds and cope with other, more sordid, matters. ("Look, Ben, *plug*; Ben say *plug*? *Plug*, Ben.") Wish vainly that James and Toby would concentrate on teaching their Trappist baby brother more suitable words. Reflect also that somebody once said, I can't recall who, but suppose it was a Frenchman, that he would be all for Democracy "mais qui videra le pot-de-chambre?" Reply, obviously, "Moi". Fear that this is the nearest I get to an intellectual thought during the morning.

Put Ben down for rest and hurry downstairs to cook lunch. Wish I could ever think of anything other than Mince to do with remains of week-end joint. People on wireless for ever suggesting splendid ideas but never can find pencil and paper in time to make note of them, and memory totally unreliable. Cookery book can only offer tiresomely over-elaborate dishes and moreover is inclined officiously to add "The wine is optional"; as far as I am concerned the whole thing is optional. Make usual mince, followed by sago pudding; cannot imagine why this is so popular with children. Spend entire meal saying Take Your Elbows off the Table, Shut your Mouth While You Are Eating, Hold Your Knife and Fork Properly, Ben, Don't do That, and Don't Encourage Him. (Good mothers don't nag.) James and Toby treat it all as normal accompaniment to intelligent mealtime conversation and discuss James' recent eye operation in imaginative detail, the latest serial in *Eagle*, and a character called Tennyson, a native, he climbed Everest with Sir Edmund Hillary.

Customary walk in afternoon follows customary route, down High Street, round the village, and home. Would love a little variety, plenty of alternative possibilities, but James and Toby implore that we stick to it and point out reasonably enough that Ben and I can go where we like in

term-time. Boys talk incessantly and very loudly and Ben forgets his Trappist role and practises singing, also very loudly. Realise too late that I meant to be a good mother and point out Beauties of Nature, Wild Flowers, Lambs . . . (no, not at this time of year now I come to think of it); have, however, as so often before, failed. Children's observations confined to Is that a Bull or a Cow, and subsequent embarrassing discussion from which I entirely dissociate myself.

*Tuesday, 11th*

Long-awaited trip to London. James and Toby immensely concerned as to What They Shall Wear, and my own sartorial problems pass comparatively unnoticed. (Only good coat and skirt definitely too tight; which looks worse, odd nylons or laddered matching ones; and do people in London wear hats these days?) Finally decide that I Will Do, and that boys definitely look nice in clean shirts and ties, and Ben engaging in tweed coat and leggings.

Despite careful planning, reach station in fearful rush at eleventh hour, train on point of departure, and are thrust by helpful porter into very end carriage in nick of time. This proves to be labelled Ladies Only, which provokes Toby to unseemly mirth and James into panic that he will be Put in Prison. Journey spent calming both and trying to dissuade Ben from crawling under seats. Tweed outfit looks steadily less and less attractive.

On arrival proceed to friend Janet's flat in Somerset Square only to find that I have forgotten number. Square is enormous and deserted, and taxi-driver is sympathetic but not unnaturally unable to help. He finally drives away shaking his head over my improvidence, as well he may, and Ben gets heavier and heavier. James runs about distractedly, and Toby takes opportunity to sit on pavement and take shoe off which he says is Broken. Am very unsympathetic indeed and beg him to get up, whereupon James suddenly shrieks There are Jeremy and Julian (sons of dear friend Janet), and so they are, both dressed in oldest and grubbiest of clothes, returning from playing with a friend. Thankfully follow them to their flat.

Janet (always so clever at school and College) presents remarkable appearance in striped tunic affair and tapered slacks, exactly like something in glossy magazine advertisements. Hair (surely used to be much darker?) scraped uncompromisingly back with wide velvet band; wonder how this would suit me but realise at once that such a style needs a better nose than I have ever possessed. She greets us with rather *distraite* effusion, flat is in state of total, but cultured, untidiness. (Flowers in vase on floor, is this very contemporary or just absent-mindedness? and remarkable picture hung low on crimson wallpaper is either very modern and clever or Janet did it herself.)

Lunch in kitchen, homely touch here but Janet succeeds in making it all seem Bohemian and arty, whereas with us it's just squalid. Food odd. (Can she have forgotten we were corning?) Hiss at Toby to eat up his peas without saying anything. He instantly says loudly that he Doesn't Like Tinned Peas. Second course, however, great success with all children as Janet has taken ingeniously simple way out of perennial What Shall we Have for Pudding problem by providing bars of chocolate all round. (Can foresee long arguments at home.) Do not really consider this a Balanced Meal but am bound to admit that Julian and Jeremy look perfectly well-nourished and are moreover much better behaved than my children.

Leave Ben to have his rest under Janet's auspices and depart with Toby and James for Madame Tussaud's.

Expedition immense success, only marred by fact that Death of Nelson tableau which boys particularly want to see is shrouded in curtains, being cleaned. Execution of Mary Queen of Scots, however, proves absorbing, and reflect, not for the first time, that my sons appear to be devoid of desirable quality of Compassion. After what feels like hours and hours of walking about and gazing, including aeons in hall devoted to Penny-in-the-Slot machines at which we spend a small fortune, but *not* Chamber of Horrors because of Toby's nightmares, decide that it Is Time To Go. Boys both assume expressions of extreme agony and say very loudly that They Must Spend Pennies First. Escort them to Gents and wait outside for ages. Finally decide that one or both have fallen down dead inside, and with some diffidence ask total stranger, just going in, if he would mind Sending the Two Little Boys Out if They Have Finished. Realise that this might have been more prettily put, but total stranger (must be a father) is kindness itself and causes J and T to emerge instantly.

Return to Janet's flat, Ben weeps at sight of us but Janet assures us he has been Very Good Up To Now (hope this is true), and we all eat enormous tea, are collected by Lee in car and get home very late. Boys instantly demand another meal, and have to be pacified with Tinned Soup in Bed.

Am quite incredibly exhausted by whole day and go to bed shortly after children.

*Wednesday, 12th*

Day wholly devoted to domestic chores. House has become incomprehensibly neglected and untidy due to one day's absence; moreover all clothes worn in London are pitch black and must be washed. Toby helps with washing and says All He Wishes is that he could Sometimes Have Clean Sheets. Am stunned and contrite, although morally certain that his complaint is unjustified, and change everybody's sheets. Realise towards lunch-time that I have not seen James for hours, and then find him propped up against Bread Bin in Larder reading very old Comic. He appears to be unaware of his whereabouts or my presence so leave him to it; can only hope this mania for reading will eventually lead to Good Books.

Spend afternoon Catching Up On Ironing, interrupted by telephone call from gloomy neighbour, Mrs Parnell, to tell me that She Has Arthritis, her Husband is in Plaster (why?) and Jenny's as Thin as a Rake. Feel I cannot let her get away with all the medical kudos and counter with James' Eye Operation. Mrs P interrupts triumphantly and yet with unabated gloom that Albert's eyes were *inoperable*. Do not attempt to continue conversation but ring off feeling quite depressed at extreme good health of my family.

At supper (baked beans and bread and cheese in kitchen), Lee says he Thinks I Ought To Have Window Above the

Sink. Agree incautiously that it Would Be Nice, and am thunderstruck when he adds casually that he will Knock a Hole in the Wall next week-end and See What Can Be Done. I beg him not to do anything so rash, and say What About Stresses and Strains? Can only hope that he will forget all about it, but know all too well that the only

Handyman jobs that dear Lee ever forgets are the ones I have particularly asked him to do.

Discuss this and other matters at length. . . . (How can we afford to send Three Sons to Boarding School, Where does all the Housekeeping Go To, How we Wish we were Rich, and Had we better give up Smoking.) Find that it is after eleven o'clock, wash up, tidy up, lay breakfast, take off apron and go to bed. Why do we have a sitting-room? We never sit in it, but it always seems to want cleaning. Suppose that we shall be calling it the Parlour next, and keeping it for Weddings and Funerals.

*Thursday, 13th*

In view of cocktail party this evening at house of Rich Unknown Neighbour, Lady Eveleigh-Anderson, waste great part of morning gloomily gazing into mirror and realising once again that I am Getting Fatter and Need a Perm. Children are encouraging and say I Am Beautiful. Feel better. Ask if they think I should Grow My Hair and Do it in a Bun. They shriek with horror and say it would be Unwomanly. Ben opens one and only box of powder and tips it over bed. All is confusion and I am very cross. Looks not improved. Eventually wash hair and do nails and realise it is long past lunch-time; at belated meal children eat vast helpings of everything and I eat nothing in frail hope that it may make me thinner. Later in afternoon am ravenous and James kindly gives me bar of chocolate which I am too weak-minded not to eat.

Get to Party rather late owing to extreme difficulty of putting children to bed and getting self and Lee ready by half-past six. (Wish people would not give parties at this impossible hour.) Baby-sitter eventually chivvies us out of house with assurances that she will read to J and T and put their light out. Walking round to Lady E-A's promise Lee that I will not talk about the Children. Or cooking, he adds.

Party very enjoyable, except that everyone I speak to asks me How Are Your Children? Lady E-A proves to be very elegant and kind with blue-rinsed hair which I admire. She says she Knew My Mother which interests me, but as it was years before I was born can think of nothing to say. She then says my Husband is Very Handsome which pleases me but can think of no rejoinder that does not sound either ungracious or conceited. She adds that He Must Be Wonderful to Live With and I wonder if she means what I think she means, and can still find nothing to answer. She concludes by saying that she is Only Speaking as an Outsider, and I instantly think of several replies none of which would be seemly. We then part, Lady E-A still unflaggingly kind but clearly feeling I am unworthy of Lee. (Am quite prepared to agree.) Feel that I do not shine as a conversationalist and that Impenetrable Silence is to shroud me for ever, but am rescued by charming American acquaintance with decanter who plies me with wine and sparkling conversation until I feel quite witty. Evening gets more and more entertaining and am just getting rather carried away in conversation with Fascinating Stranger who is an Artist, on whom I am sufficiently merry to inflict my views on Matisse (whose pictures I have never set eyes on), when Lee appears and hisses at me that Everyone Seems to be Going.

Having left, realise that it is Only Half-past Eight, that we are both thoroughly in the Party Mood, and decide that it would be a terrible waste of the baby-sitter to go home yet, and after much discussion ring up the Sinclairs, friends in neighbouring village, from telephone box, and ask if we can Come Round. Do, says Felicity S, but we are Just Eating, Give us Forty-Five Minutes. Lee then fetches car (hoping baby-sitter will not hear and think we are Thieves) and discovers that it is nearly Out of Petrol and that he has No Money so that we can neither drive about to pass the time nor go to a pub. Drive to Sinclairs' village as slowly as possible and discover we still have half an hour to wait, no alternative but to sit in car outside the S's drive gates and wait for time to pass which it does with incredible slowness. Party Mood ebbs. Lee says it would be All Very Well if we weren't Married.

*Friday, 14th*
Washing has once again reached astronomical proportions and must be done; sheets and towels fearful nuisance to dry but cannot afford to send them to the laundry. Try (as always) to do wash *and* clean entire house before lunch and (as always) realise that it is impossible. Children play in garden in lovely sunshine and complain at lunch that they Wish they lived in London, that they Do Not Like Fish (both eat second helpings of cod with gusto nonetheless), and that they Never Seem to Get Any Presents. This last fantastically untrue as both have enormous toy-cupboards overflowing with expensive toys given them by doting grandparents. Contemplate short homily on Counting

One's Blessings but do not deliver it, as am well aware that this would be complete waste of time, and am moreover fully occupied with Ben who is Spitting.

Hear talk on wireless in afternoon by lady who Keeps Goats; she says they Cut Down Your Milk Bills and Keep the Garden Tidy. Resolve to keep goats.

*Saturday, 15th*
Lee has morning off and spirit of holiday descends. He takes all three children into garden after breakfast and I think about What we shall Have for Lunch. Joint today and cold meat tomorrow easier; joint tomorrow more traditional, but then what do we have today? Am thinking about *soufflé* (which I cannot make) and finishing washing-up, when fearful clatter inside wall by my head startles me appallingly and point of chisel, preceded by quite large lump of plaster, bursts into room three inches from my temple. Am about to break into impassioned complaint and abuse when J and T rush into kitchen screeching with excitement and asking if I Like My New Window? Lee and Ben follow, Lee not what I consider very apologetic about my narrow escape, and I am begged to Come Outside and See. Cannot be so churlish as to refuse, and find in outside wall quite large cavity (rather reminiscent of the dentist) where New Window is to be. Lee continues to hack and bang at it with various lethal weapons (more like dentist than ever), bricks, stones and rubble fall out and are enthusiastically collected by children (what for?), and opening into kitchen gradually widens until we can look at one another through it. (Mess in sink by this stage quite

indescribable.) Admit that window *when finished* should be great success, providing entire wall does not collapse. Lee says it will be Finished by Lunch-time, he is just Going into Town to Buy the Glass. Make no comment on this other than to beg him to take children with him.

Reflect how odd it is that Lee, who has been doing this Do It Yourself business for quite a long time now, and is into the bargain an intelligent man, is totally unable to assess how long any job will take him. Am prepared to bet that he won't be back with glass until lunch-time and that window won't be finished this week-end. Only hope it won't rain. *Later.* Window is not finished by lunch-time nor by supper-time either, and it *does* rain. Lee fixes up dirty old piece of sacking across gaping hole, which now looks like bomb damage, and praises himself immoderately. I think of all the men I might have married.

*Sunday, 16th*
Get up very late and have fearful rush getting breakfast cooked, eaten and washed up, and most of lunch organised before taking James to church. During service he drops prayer book three times and collection twice but is otherwise good. Sermon is beyond his comprehension but he passes time scrutinising, with deepest attention, small printed card which he finds in his pocket. Cannot quite make out what this is until we get up for the hymn when I recognise it as souvenir from Madame Tussaud's penny-in-the-slot machines entitled "How Much Sex Appeal Do You Register?"

Outside church meet Susan, dressed as usual like front cover of *Vogue*, and looking much younger than me which is aggravating. She takes me on one side and hisses that she thinks she is going to Have a Baby, but I am not to tell anyone as she Isn't Sure Yet. (She has told me she is going to have a baby approximately once a month since I have known her, but nothing more is ever heard of it.) Endeavour to sound surprised and congratulatory. Offer use of pram, carrycot, baby bath, etc. All is spurned by Susan who says Naturally she will get All That from Harrods. Naturally. Am inclined to forget, occasionally, that Susan, who has rich parents, wealthy husband and, as yet, no children, and endless supply of domestic help into the bargain, sees life very differently from me. Say this, more or less, and Susan replies that I am Quite Wonderful, but that she could never Manage Like Me as her husband could never Live in Chaos. Not even in Organised Chaos, she adds kindly. This annoys me and also reminds me that lunch is probably burning in oven, retrieve James from contemplation of tombstones and hurry home to Organised Chaos.

*Monday, 17th*
Wholly unprecedented and unexpected telephone call from *Daily Tabard* to ask Whether I would Write an Article for them? Ask dazedly Why Me? Quickly add that I will certainly write article, without even asking what it is to be about. *Daily Tabard* says mysteriously that It has Been Given My Name, as Housewife who Writes. Writing hitherto been confined to totally unsuccessful bombardment of editors with articles and subsequent collection of Rejection Slips, but just retain enough sanity to refrain from telling the *D. T.* this, pull myself together and ask for further information about article. Oh, says *D. T.* (voice young, female, and transatlantic), she guesses she had better come and talk to me about it. Point out that it is a long way for her to come, but she is airy about this and says she will Be With Me around Eleven. Can only suppose she is accustomed to American Speed of Travel, but tell her name of nearest town with station and say I will meet her there. Ring off in complete stupor and try to feel like Real Writer. Children are agog and say that I will soon be Famous, and absolutely refuse to be despatched to Mrs Parnell for duration of visit from the Press. Finally compromise by extorting promise that they will stay in the garden; and not look through window either, I add hastily.

Quite unable to settle to anything while waiting for *Daily Tabard* to arrive, until it occurs to me wildly that she may Take My Photograph and even if she doesn't I am not Fit to Be Seen anyway.

Waiting becomes agonising, finally start lunch, where-upon phone rings and rather exhausted American voice says Well, she finally got to my town. Leave James and Toby with strict instructions to finish their puddings and look after Ben, and drive one mile into town. Quite easy to identify *Daily Tabard* as everyone else in sight at station is known to me. Pick her up (rather ashamed of shabby little car, but Lee's much worse), and we go home. *Daily Tabard* proves to be charming, joins us for remains of lunch, is great success with children, and helps me put Ben down for rest.

Settle ourselves with coffee and cigarettes in drawing-room (flowers died last week, pity I forgot to remove them), and *Daily Tabard* says Well, and embarks on long discussion about Series of Feature Articles on Sex Instruction for children in England and America, and how nice it would be if I were to give the point of view of the Typical English Housewife. Do not at all care for this epithet, but am in no position to quibble and suppose it is accurate anyway, and agree to everything. Recall several remarkable reactions by James and Toby on being told the Facts of Life, recount these and *Daily Tabard* says they are Just the Thing. Ask if she would like photographs of J and T and she says That Would Be Cute, but does nothing further about it. Finally take her back to train for London, and drive home reflecting that *Daily Tabard* ought to be able to pay handsomely if they are so light-hearted with their finances as to send employee on long two-way journey for so unimportant an object. (Unimportant to them anyway.)

Later in the day, they ring up again (further evidence of extreme wealth in this airy disregard of telephone bills) to confirm commission to write article, about 800 words, and Would Fifteen Guineas Suit Me. Am absolutely staggered, accept hoarsely and eagerly and ring off quick before they can change their minds.

Spend evening writing article, asking Lee's advice on it, rewriting it and planning how to spend fifteen guineas. Finally settle on a piano, a Bendix washing machine, a rotary ironer, and an extra week's summer holiday. Lee enters fully into the spirit of the thing and says What about Eton for James? Know very well it will in point of fact if it ever materialises be used to Help Out the Housekeeping, but am still elated.

### Tuesday, 18th

Perfect drying day. (Weather assessed by me nowadays purely in terms of suitability for laundry.) B.B.C. issues solemn warning about gales in or around Dogger Minch and Skye . . . or something . . . but feel that these, if they reach me, will be beneficial rather than otherwise. It further adds in awed tones that South Cones are Being Hoisted somewhere or other; wonder idly what they are and why they are always being hoisted, never *in situ* or even being lowered?

Do washing and think it looks picturesque blowing in wind. (Aesthetic sense showing faint symptoms of renaissance?)

View larder shelves in terms of lunch and find that we have run out of practically everything, and realise that shopping expedition is unavoidable. Housework gets left once again, send James and Toby upstairs to get tidy while I do my best with self and Ben. Screech upstairs to boys to Wash their Knees, and when they come down have to point out that of course I meant their Faces too, and send them upstairs all over again. Fearful fight ensues of which I do not attempt to ascertain the cause but bundle both into car and set off. They mutter a good deal but finally subside and town is reached, and I deliver tremendous lecture on necessity of Behaving Well in Shops.

They behave abominably in all shops.

Climax is reached in hardware shop where I am trying to

buy birthday present for Lee. (Very expensive Do-It-Yourself gadget that looks like powerful pistol powered by electricity.) Shop assistant, who looks like Peter Ustinov, says Which Component do I want with it? Have no idea. Ask him which would be most useful; he says Well there's this one, it makes very good egg-cups. Assure him that we have plenty of egg-cups. Undeterred, he says Or candlesticks? Repudiate candlesticks also, and say that it's More for Odd Jobs Round the House. Peter Ustinov looks hunted, and says defensively that it *does* make *very good* egg-cups, and I am just about to interrupt before he can go on about candlesticks again when Maternal Instinct makes me look round for boys. James is halfway up small step-ladder, Toby is nowhere to be seen and Ben is kicking at display table idiotically heavily laden with ovenware. Frown and shake head fiercely at James as he is out of hearing of anything but absolute bellow, and snatch Ben away just as large casserole is beginning to rock. He roars, and James comes away from step-ladder arguing bitterly. Tell Peter Ustinov that I Will Come Back Another Day, and he says he Thinks the Other Little Boy is in the Paint Store. He kindly goes and extracts Toby and we leave the shop in disorder, followed by superior smiles from customers who have had the sense to leave their children at home.

Halfway home Toby produces small tin of Dove-grey Gloss Paint and says innocently Won't Daddy be pleased? Am horrified and tell him that by Six years Old he ought to know What is Stealing and What Isn't. Cannot however face going back and decide to ring up shop from home and have pot of paint put on already enormous account.

Is Toby embryo Juvenile Delinquent?

On arrival home he avoids further recrimination owing to the—for him—fortunate fact that washing has all fallen down in the mud. B.B.C. evidently quite right about gales, South Cones and all.

Much later, at children's bathtime, Ben becomes wild and uncontrollable and eventually takes apparently fatal plunge under water. Toby with great presence of mind rescues him, and I congratulate him and tell him that People have Won Medals for Less. Later still, when I take final look at children before going to bed, am much moved to observe large irregularly cut-out piece of cardboard pinned on to his pyjama jacket with nappy-pin.

*Wednesday, 19th*
James and Toby due to return to small day school tomorrow, both are delighted (great tribute to school, or perhaps poor reflection on home background?), and I spend much time looking out tidy grey shirts and shorts, retrieving their Work Books from the bottom of the toy-cupboards, cleaning their ears, washing their hair, and cutting their nails. (Home background, now I come to think of it, almost certainly not up to par, as so much time and energy has to be expended before J and T are fit to appear in public.)

Have also to cope in evening with Portable Lunches for both, as school does not provide hot meal but is willing to Warm Things Up. Remember vividly absolute inability during last term to think of anything except Cottage Pie and Fish Pie, followed by Blanc-mange in jar, and quite see

21

that same difficulty is about to descend on me all over again. Make two little cottage pies and two little blanc-manges in jars, and wish unavailingly that someone would invent fireproof dish that is unbreakable.

Ask Lee if he thinks we should keep goats. He says That would be Splendid but that I must Milk them Myself. Adds that he will Make a Shelter for them. Would very much rather buy one, but cannot hurt Lee's feelings, so thank him and say that I will get the goats when shelter materialises. He says that he will make shelter when I Get Goats. Deadlock appears to be reached, but compromise by saying that I will ask Mrs Parnell, always mine of informa-tion about everybody's activities, who she thinks would sell me goats and teach me to milk them. Lee says disgustedly That Woman (very unfair, he has never exchanged two words with Mrs P) and continues to wedge rather shaky little piece of wood on to top of home-made window. I say, quoting current advertisement (I think for Building Society), That Finial's Not Plumb. This is not at all a suc-cess, window evidently giving trouble, Lee gets hot and bothered and says Plasterers and Builders much more skilled than he had hitherto realised. Am sorry for him, but nevertheless have to bite back inclination to say I told you so.

### Thursday, 20th

James and Toby off to school after familiar argument as to whether they should Wear their House-shoes and Take their gumboots or Wear their Lace-ups and Keep them on. Lee finally takes them off in car and I decide to Get the house Straight after the Holidays. This plan utterly frustrated by Ben who obviously misses J and T, although their attentions frequently reduce him to wails, and who pesters me with remarkable tenacity. Finally take him out in push-chair, and meet Mrs Parnell at crossroads. She walks home with me and I ask her about Goats. She says in astonishment Why ever do I want to keep goats? I explain about milk bills and keeping garden tidy. She says, gloomy as ever, that they Smell Terrible and we won't have a Flower Left. What I really want, she adds bossily and quite incorrectly, is to Keep Chicken. (Why chicken in the singular? Does she mean just one, or is this hitherto unknown technical expression, like Grouse, or even Sheep?) Evidently the latter, as she goes on to explain immense financial benefits of keeping large numbers of Chicken, at negligible capital outlay and mentions light-heartedly a sum that I could in no way raise or borrow even if I liked chickens. Chicken. Finally I get her off the subject and she reverts to customary gloom and says Pigs are a Problem. I daresay they are, but I do not want to keep pigs. Does she, I ask firmly, know anyone who Keeps

Goats? (Gate reached by this time, and Ben getting restive, am dying to go in but still hopeful of receiving helpful information.)

Mrs P comes out into the open and says Yes, Mrs Somebody, cannot hear name but do not want to delay matters further by saying What? she lives in next village and Shows Goats. I say thank you very much, I will get in touch with her. Mrs P much shocked by this casual approach and says reprovingly that she will Ring Up Mrs Somebody (Mrs Senna? Surely not) and see if she will See Me. Take instant dislike to Mrs Senna, and think she sounds very high-hat, but too late to withdraw as Mrs P has become very managing and says she will Arrange Everything. Thank her, rather falsely as I now wish I had not mentioned the beastly goats at all, and take Ben indoors not a moment too soon.

*Friday, 21st*

Ben more reconciled to absence of J and T and I plan immense programme of housework. Put on jeans, which do not suit me but are quite invaluable for scrambling activities concerned with Cleaning Picture Rails, tie up hair in scarf, and immerse myself. At about two o'clock when I am completely filthy and exhausted and have just decided stop for Cup of Tea instead of lunch (Ben has had his out of tins and is now asleep), doorbell rings. Discover on doorstep ex-boy-friend, not seen since student days, with hitherto unknown wife and infant. They look astonished, as well they may, but I say graciously Come In, and How nice to see them. (A Lady can Still Look a Lady Whatever

25

she is Wearing. Only hope this old saw is really reliable, as
am banking heavily on it.)

Ex-boy-friend, Charles, has grown little beard and is
working with distinguished opera company, but is otherwise unchanged. Wife, introduced as Julia, is beautifully

dressed and made-up, and has a figure that infuriates me.
She is either very shy or dislikes me on sight (or maybe I
have halitosis?), as she keeps her head averted from me
throughout the visit and mutters inaudibly. Infant, about
eighteen months, is stout and stares at me unwinkingly but
neither moves nor speaks. Very unlike either of its parents,
as Charles is as voluble as ever. He chats lightly about
Brecht, the Swedish cinema, several newly-issued books
that I have not heard of, and American violinist Tossy
Spivakovsky, whose playing he much admires. Reflect sadly
that I used to be able to keep up with this sort of conversation, but have to admit that nowadays I am a bit Out of
Touch; here Julia interjects, head still averted and can barely

hear it, something about My Wonderful Gift, and Wicked Waste. Suppose she is referring to rather meagre Wedding present conferred on them by Lee and me, and think her language excessive, but she goes on to say slightly more audibly that I ought to be doing something with my Talents. (If she means my literary activities, should like to refer her to *Daily Tabard*.) Wrong again, it transpires that she means my Acting. Am staggered, but remember that in long ago student days I did take part in play produced by Charles. At this point he agrees that I Ought to be On the Stage, but I do not think he really means it, as he is as aware as I am that build most kindly described as Junoesque is not the greatest asset in Modern Drama. Before he can perjure himself further, infant creates disturbance by becoming fretful, and I offer Orange juice. Julia becomes embarrassed, and much more human and likeable, and confesses that infant is resolutely attached to bottle and refuses all other liquid. Am far too well accustomed to the spirit of cast-iron determination frequently manifested by the very young to be as shocked about this as she evidently expects me to be, and she says Well, if I'm sure I don't mind, and produces bottle. (Should never be surprised to learn that it contains neat gin.) Infant retires with it into corner and sits with it clenched between teeth rather like an old man with a pipe. Am impressed by this expression of will-power, and say that He Will Go Far. At this Charles and Julia both turn into quite ordinary parents and tell me a great deal about infant's activities, creditable and otherwise, and I go and fetch Ben who is awake and shrieking, and get in my fair share of boasting about him. (Only wish Ben, on being shown to strangers, would not bury his face with such idiotic coyness in my bosom, and show clinging and grizzling characteristics quite out of keeping with normal behaviour.)

Charles and Julia finally take infant away, bottle still clamped in jaws, Charles saying as he goes that we must all Do a Show in London some time. I am enthusiastic, but add hastily Nothing too Intellectual, please. He looks thoughtfully at me for a long time and finally pronounces that He thinks he can get Tickets for popular Musical Comedy. Feel he has gauged my present mental level with depressing accuracy, and can only be thankful he didn't suggest *Noddy in Toyland*. Wave to departing car with mixed feelings, and have tendency to relapse into great state of self-pity about My Wasted Life, when James and Toby return from school in friends' car and embrace me with such affection that I recover instantly and give them chocolate, at which they are both astonished and delighted.

*Saturday, 22nd*
Spend morning as usual cleaning and cooking. (Why do yesterday's housewifely activities seem to have resulted in increase of dirt and dust rather than reverse?) Interrupted incessantly by children and also by several telephone calls. Hope each time that it is *Daily Tabard* to tell me how good they think my article is, and to commission several more at similar vast rate of pay, but they remain silent. Instead Mrs Parnell rings to say she has Talked to Mrs Senna about me, and that Mrs S will See me this afternoon. (Sounds more condescending than ever, should never be surprised if she

offered me an Audience, but must beware of being prejudiced against her at this stage, and must moreover
endeavour to find out her real name.) Say unwillingly that
if Lee is not called out I can manage this afternoon, but Mrs
P evidently takes my co-operation for granted and ignores
this, and goes on to assure me that she has told Mrs Senna
that I am a Good Worker. Do not at all care for this phrase
which makes me feel like a scullery maid applying for a job,
but before I can point out that it is advice on goats that I
want rather than permission to keep them, Mrs P embarks
on long story about further ailments of her family and
shows tendency to ask What my Husband thinks about
Jenny's State of Health. Discourage this, knowing all too
well Lee's reaction to being asked to treat other people's
patients over the telephone, and say that he is not That Sort
of Doctor. (Add, with humorous intent, "I'm not that Sort
of Girl", but Mrs P does not see the point.)

Telephone rings again and is answered by James who
says fiercely Who Are You? into mouthpiece and then
What? fifteen times. I snatch instrument from him before
he entirely antagonises caller (*Daily Tabard*?), and it turns
out to be old friend Hermione, not seen for years and
years. She is staying nearby for a wedding, and would so
much like to see me before returning to Inverness. Am
delighted, and arrange for her to come and stay on
Monday. (Only hope I can find some un-torn sheets for
spare-room bed, and that H likes children.)

Just as lunch is on table and I am summoning family to
come and eat it (at which, as usual, they all remember
important things they have to do elsewhere), phone rings

yet again and it is Susan. She is sorry to bother me but is it true that I Write? (Tone sounds as though she puts this somewhere between addiction to marijuana, and incest.) I say deprecatingly Well yes, a bit. In that case, she says, will I come to coffee next Wednesday as she has invited newly arrived neighbour who has written a book and does not know what to talk to her about. She is, she adds, a *divorcée*. (Feel that that should give us plenty of material for conversation, but perhaps this attitude unsympathetic and do not mention it.) Agree to come to coffee if I may bring Ben, and Hermione if she is still staying with me, and ask What about the Baby? Oh says Susan in harrassed tones, It's all Very Difficult. Cannot imagine what she means, either she is going to have a baby or she isn't, but she is unwilling to explain and rings off. Shall give her one of Lee's revolting textbooks on the subject if there is much more of this.

James says at lunch What is a *Divorcée*? (Really must discourage him from listening in to phone calls over upstairs extension.) Explain that sometimes people's husbands turn out to be selfish and unkind and leave their wives, to which he replies thoughtfully that it is Not a Very Nice Thing to Do to a Lady. Feel that he has put the matter in a nutshell.

In afternoon go to see Mrs Senna. Find her farm with some difficulty, it turns out to be a vast establishment rather like a ranch in a film, all white railings and red roofs, very attractive, and discover Mrs Senna, also rather like something in a film, very decorative in linen slacks surrounded by enchanting prancing goats and kids. We greet one another warily and I receive distinct impression that she was as ready to dislike me as I was her, evidently Mrs P has genius for presenting her acquaintances in unfavourable light to each other. Mutual mistrust overcome however and we get on very well. She gives me much helpful advice about care of goats, including obstetric details which I hope fervently never to have to put into practice. She gives me small glass of goat's milk to drink, which I do, and find it excellent. Am quite confirmed in intention to keep goats, and ask her about prices. She appals me by saying that You can Pay up to Fifty for a Good Nanny. Early upbringing (Never show any emotion about Money) restrains me from blenching, and I manage, I think, to appear unmoved but whole question of goats will quite clearly have to be reconsidered. Remainder of conversation is entirely bogus as far as I am concerned, although Mrs Senna relents so far as to admit that an inferior Nanny *can* sometimes be picked up for a mere Twenty. Feel inwardly convinced that this is all great nonsense, and that Mrs S just views life and finance from pinnacles of wealth far remote from me, but do not really know enough about subject to be confident.

Return home to find that Lee has finished new window in kitchen and I am called upon to admire it, which I do. Cannot resist pointing out that it looks exactly like wartime machine-gun slits in pill-boxes; Lee agrees and is amused but James and Toby profoundly offended and much time has to be spent reassuring them that I really *do* like window, and that I think Daddy is very clever.

Later on we prepare to go out to cinema, baby-sitter arrives and is astonished at window. She finally pronounces that Upon her Word, my Husband is Too Clever to be a Doctor. Fortunately Lee takes this in the spirit in which it is meant and is gratified, and says it is the Best Compliment he has Ever Had.

*Sunday, 23rd*

Do not take James to church, and he asks Why. Reply thoughtlessly that it is the fourth Sunday in the month and the Vicar always has some Comic Capers on this date. Lee points out rather curtly that this is a poor way to refer to Sung Eucharist and I am abashed. (Nevertheless, feel strongly that this is a form of service totally unsuited to rural congregation that does not have a choir.) Become involved, in the evening, in quite frightful discussion with Lee concerning children's education. He becomes immersed in fearful calculations, as a result of which he announces, a shade pontifically, that We Have Three Sons. Point out rather acidly that I am well aware of this, after all I produced them. He begs me to stick to serious matter in hand (very unfair, the actual production of sons or daughters either for that matter exceedingly serious matter for their producer, but restrain myself from obstetrical reminiscences and endeavour to pay attention to further utterances). Very well then, says Lee, he has just worked out the total cost of educating three sons, *excluding* University, and finds the result to be Seven Thousand Five Hundred pounds. This is so far beyond possibility or even reason that I am unable to do anything except laugh insanely. Lee is annoyed, and says *will* I listen. I do listen, and he adds that he may have made a slight misjudgement of a thousand pounds more or less but he can't see that it makes much difference. After what feels like hours and hours of discussion as to how we can economise (no more frozen vegetables, marge instead of butter, give up smoking, no holidays *ever*), we reach conclusion which has been perfectly apparent all along, that we cannot afford it. Lee then says that We must not be Snobbish, and after all they ought to be able to pass the Eleven Plus exam and go to Grammar School. Am seriously torn at this stage between maternal conviction that my children are far cleverer than anyone else's and equal certainty that they will never be able to pass *any* exam. Feel anyway tremendous prejudice against Eleven Plus exam which I have always understood to be designed for the glorification of The Crossword Mind . . . but realise that we must bow to the inevitable, and sadly relinquish dreams of prep and public schools. Make final not very hopeful suggestion that Perhaps something will Turn Up; but Lee replies grimly that It will have to be a Miracle, and sits down there and then to cancel James' name for entry to excellent prep school next term. Go to bed in state of extreme gloom, reflecting sadly how undemocratic we really are at heart.

*Monday, 24th*
Arrival of Hermione does much to restore morale. She is as entertaining as ever and does nothing but tell us all how wonderful we are, which makes us think highly of her intelligence, taste, and judgement. She proves moreover to be the perfect guest in that she quite automatically helps with everything but never once tells me much better ways of doing anything. Ask her whether she thinks I should keep goats, and she says Wouldn't they be a bit of a

nuisance? which so exactly fits in with what I am beginning to think myself that strongly supported by her I finally jettison all idea of goats. Very relieved. Look, however, at the garden and realise that If no goats then I must Do something about the weeds, which now eclipse every flower in the place. At H's instigation (really remarkably brilliant adviser, wish she didn't live in Inverness), ring up nearby Horticultural College and ask if they can send over An Expert to tell me what to do about garden. Slight misunderstanding here, as they evidently envisage large estate to be given Capability Brown treatment, and I have to say No no, just ordinary flower beds and things. Horticultural College seems surprised and says Well what do I want to know? Everything, I confess, I don't know what any of the flowers are, nor how to treat them, we haven't lived here very long. (This perhaps not strictly true but have not sufficient moral courage to tell them for how long in fact I have entirely neglected garden.) Eventually Horticultural College agree to send someone over tomorrow morning, but they sound rather unenthusiastic. Feel disheartened, had expected them to leap to the rescue of ill-used flowers rather like floral version of N.S.P.C.C. but suppose that they can't really believe that anyone is as much of a fool about flowers as in fact I am.

After tea it rains and we play horrible game, much loved by James and Toby, Peter Rabbit Race Game, in which dice is thrown on floor at least fifty times and Toby loses his temper every time he has to Miss Two Turns. Game is further complicated by Ben, indignant at not being included, who hangs about table and tries to snatch dice board, counters, and Peter Rabbit and Co until in despair I give up my place (Jemima Puddleduck) and take him to bed. Hermione heroically finishes game, very cleverly contriving not to win herself, and I realise not for the first time that James and Toby behave very much better with everyone else than they do with me, as playroom once I have left it resounds with happy laughter and never a shriek.

*Tuesday, 25th*
At what seems like crack of dawn front door bell rings and young woman from Horticultural College is revealed. Have only just got Lee and boys off and have been chatting over remains of breakfast with Hermione and am moreover still in shabby old dressing-gown. House looks terrible and so do I and am ashamed. Hermione however copes efficiently, shows young woman into sitting-room (tidy?) and says We will be with her in a minute. Due to fantastic rushings about and not washing (must never tell Toby this) we are with her in not much more than a minute. Grand tour of garden ensues. Young Woman, says her name is Miss Englefield, is kind about everything and says we ought to be able to make something out of it. Fear Capability Brown touch emerging and say All I want is to be told names of flowers and what to do about them, and produce piece of paper and pencil in what I hope is business-like way. Miss E then tells me a great many names, most of which I cannot spell, and adds sometimes You ought to Prune this, and sometimes I shouldn't Touch That. Get notes very muddled. Ask What about this, and indicate rather pretty little creeping flower that I think looks well. Miss E says Oh

that stuff, it is a nuisance isn't it, terrible to get rid of, and I try to pretend I knew it was a weed all along. (Am well aware that Hermione is not deceived by this.) Miss E then comes to a sudden halt rather like a pointer dog and gasps in astonished admiration in front of meagre little bush that I have never even noticed before, and says Surely not a Carborundum Mysterioso (or something), crawls excitedly round it like Sherlock Holmes looking for clues, and finally admits that it is a Carborundum Mysterioso and we obviously go up by leaps and bounds in her estimation. Regard meagre little bush with increased respect and a certain amount of alarm. Ask what special treatment it requires,

have visions of having to wrap it up in cotton-wool every night, but Miss E says firmly that It is Quite Hardy, and continues to gaze at it admiringly. Still think weed is prettier, but do not say so. We then skirt Compost Heap, at which Miss E sniffs ecstatically, and nasty patch of what looks like open-cast mining on a small scale which is all that remains of James' recent efforts to Dig a Swimming Pool; at this Miss E stops and suggests that it would be a good place for a rockery, but I have vision of still more fiddling about with plants and weeds than I already see in store for me, and make long impassioned speech about how much I dislike rockeries. Miss E does not press the point, but later as she is leaving and I thank her for all her help she says she hopes she has been some use, but that it isn't really much in her line, as her speciality is Rockeries. Feel that she has had the last word.

When Lee comes home he is impressed at hearing of expert's visit, and asks to be told all she has said. I show him highly rare and valuable little bush, and he says It doesn't Look Much. (My own sentiments exactly, but am depressed to notice as so often before how much more honest Lee is than I; wonder if this is a male characteristic or is it just that I am depraved?) He then asks What about the other things, what ought we to be pruning? and I find I have lost the notes I so conscientiously took. Memory is no help at all, even Hermione fails me and says she knows there was *something* that had to be pruned this month, and Lee has much to say about my inefficiency. Cannot really blame him (though naturally do not admit as much to him).

*Wednesday, 26th*

Prevail upon Hermione to stay another day, and we gallop through chores (which to my astonishment I find quite enjoyable performed *a deux*; maybe it's solitude rather than domesticity which makes housewifery such a bore?) and take Ben and go to have coffee with Susan. Promised guest, writer and *divorcee*, is there, and not at all what we had expected. Do not really know what we *had* expected, except vague idea of sophistication and wicked knowingness, but on the contrary she is meek and rather shy and has dimples and curly hair and we all get on very well. Conversation, far from being literary, is exclusively concerned with Mothers-In-Law, and many startling facts are produced. *Divorcée*, Ruth, confesses in tones of restrained indignation, that when her husband left her her mother-in-law said it was All Ruth's Fault and that her son had been Perfect until he married her. No one else can quite compete with this but Susan does her best with complaints that do not sound to me really justifiable; *her* mother-in-law she says will *give* her things, horrible but expensive things, that she doesn't know what to do with. Find it quite difficult not to interrupt eagerly with suggestion that she should hand unwanted gifts on to me, occupy myself instead with Ben and biscuit crumbs and take no further part in conversation. Hardly worth taking part in anyway as it is rapidly becoming a shouting match between Susan and her other guests, even Hermione to my surprise joining in with wild tales about unnamed friends whom I suspect of being wholly fictitious. Reflect that perhaps we are fortunate in being spared the In-Law problem, and also, more gloomily, that being a successful mother-in-law is obviously next door to an impossibility and that I had better make up my mind here and now to go away and shoot myself the day after Ben's wedding.

Before we leave, manage to have some conversation with Ruth, ask her about her book and congratulate her on it. She is charmingly modest and adroitly turns conversation to my writing, and I am nearly flattered into showing off about it, but luckily remember in time that I am talking to a Real Writer, and restrict myself to telling her about the *Daily Tabard*, about which she is encouraging, and says Now I have got my Foot In. (Only hope foot is seen, that's all, and not just trodden on.) We arrange to meet again, and Hermione and I depart with Ben (biscuit crumbs from head to foot), and we discuss everyone cosily all the way home.

*Thursday, 27th*
Departure of Hermione to everyone's regret, she assures us that she will come again and begs us to come and see her in Inverness. Many wild promises made under stress of emotion, only wish any of them ever likely to materialise. She goes off with Lee and boys after breakfast, to be dropped at station, and I go upstairs to do her room and find that she has left behind small hat, torch and propelling pencil. Absolutely impossible to pack these together or singly, feel temporarily far less pro-Hermione and get on with chores.

Second post brings letter from headmaster of prep school now destined *not* to receive James and Toby. Headmaster is, he says, very disappointed that Our Boys are not to come to him. (Why? Have half a mind to tell him he ought to be giving great sighs of relief.) Is there not, headmaster continues, some way round the difficulty? Are there for instance any concessions he could make? (Feel much inclined to say Yes, if he let both boys off paying any fees at all we might be able to manage to pay for Ben in six years' time.) However, feel touched by letter and grateful for kind intentions shown in it, but know all too well that Lee when he comes home will say that it is still Out of the Question. (As indeed he does, with a rider about Will I please not open his letters. Point out that I don't normally, but thought this one looked interesting, which is, as he points out, a very poor reason.)

Decide to do some Bottling, which is an activity I have hitherto avoided, and pick large quantities of rhubarb and belated gooseberries. Slave away for hours in the kitchen, Topping and Tailing, Sterilising, making Syrup, only to find that I have miscalculated amount of fruit required and have to dash out into garden to collect more at a critical moment. Rhubarb patch unfortunately at far end of garden and I have to rush past Lee, who is mowing. He is astonished but I have no time to explain. Most unfortunately process has to be repeated more than once as I continue to have too much syrup and too little fruit, and I become hot and exhausted. Lee shrieks with laughter and says he didn't know Bottling was such an Athletic sport, very funny, only wish he would stop playing about with lawn mower and come and do some picking himself, but when I suggest this he becomes smug and masculine and says Bottling is Women's Work, for which I could willingly kill him, and disappears in a cloud of foul-smelling petrol and deafening roar.

*Friday, 28th*
By quite incredible coincidence letter arrives from aged female relation of Lee's at Torquay asking after the dear children and saying in casual sort of way that she supposes James will be off to school soon and of course she will meet all expenses. Lee and I read letter about ten times and have great difficulty in believing any of it. Whole future looks completely different, we hastily rearrange all our ideas about village school and Eleven Plus and Lee promises to write to Headmaster tonight. Write myself to Great-Aunt Elizabeth in tones of almost hysterical gratitude; am only sorry that powers of expression are limited and feel she will never really know extent of our appreciation.

Children on being told of bright future are more or less unmoved, James says Oh Good then he can write with a proper pen; and Toby says he had always *intended* to go to boarding school; he is, he says, going to this prep school, Ashley House, then to Rugby and then to Magdalen. Am rather impressed with his powers of prophecy and only hope they will continue to be justified. Meanwhile point out that So much excitement has made everyone very late as it is already after nine o'clock and they all depart hastily.

Spend remainder of day in blissful dream, but am disconcerted to observe in myself tendency to be more impressed by the fact that I am going to be a Real Prep School Mother than by James' good fortune. Apparently even Motherhood cannot entirely overcome real ingrained egotism. Telephone rings constantly, once it is Lee saying Is it Really True? Once it is Mrs Senna saying she has heard of a Nice Nannie in Milk and am I interested? Am too much of a moral coward to say outright No not at all, but temporise and say Well I think we'd better wait until we've got Suitable Accommodation. Mrs S, not deceived, laughs and says rather nicely Have I got cold feet? I come out into the open and say Yes I have. Well, well never mind, she replies, she can easily find a home for the poor little thing, and rings off leaving me feeling heartless. Final call is from Lady E-A who organises local amateur theatricals. She has heard, she says, that my charming husband Acts. Yes, he does or used to. Am just about to tell her about my own dramatic activities when she cuts me firmly short and says Handsome young men are so *rare*, *do* I think he would join them? She has a lovely part for him, a foreign nobleman, he could just *be himself*. Well, I don't know, I say, I can't answer for him, but he does like acting. She then adds kindly that she's got a little Part for me too, but this evidently by the way, as she then goes on again for a long time about Lee and his Lovely Deep Velvety Voice. Never noticed it myself. At last I say that I will get him to ring her, and she rings off. Can quite see that Lee will have a lovely time if he decides to join up with Lady E-A and her troupe but am not too sure of what my position will be.

Fetch children from school and take opportunity to tell teacher of James' good fortune. She is generously delighted and says she will be sorry to lose him but that We Deserve some Good Luck. Feel like a waif and stray who has been rescued . . . which in a way I rather am.

*Saturday, 29th*

Week-end occupied largely about garden. Owing to fact that I have with customary efficiency lost little piece of paper with gardening expert's instructions on it I am unable to tell Lee what we ought to be doing about anything; all I can remember is that she said we ought to prune some things but leave others severely alone; Lee is not as annoyed about this as he justifiably might be, but takes instead the line that there is something rather touching about my feminine help-lessness, which annoys me intensely. Retire to particularly prickly gooseberry bush and prune that with more energy than skill to relieve my feelings and am rapidly being torn to ribbons and covered with tattoo-like patterns of thorns when wild shrieks of excitement from Lee (always so calm) send me hotfoot to the log-pile, expecting to find one or both of the boys with broken legs. Far from it. All are gathered excitedly round gazing at small ancient walnut which Toby has found on the ground. Look—look—look, says Lee hysterically, three hundred pounds at *least*. Can only suppose that he has gone clean off his head and ask rather grumpily what he is making such a fuss about? Walnuts, he says, don't I see what that means, a walnut *tree*. Begin to feel rather like the Mole having things kindly explained to him by Ratty and indicate coldly that that's obvious and I still don't see. Lee interrupts and says that on *The Archers* (radio serial to which he is passionately addicted) it said that a walnut tree was worth hundreds of pounds. Feelings undergo wholehearted change and become as excited as anyone and we all search madly for walnut tree amongst overgrown spinney where walnut was found. Finally identify it, and lose ourselves in happy dreams about spending of enormous sums of money. I am in favour of completely remodelled kitchen, Aga cooker and Bendix washing machine. Lee urges a new car. James and Toby with one voice ask if now we can have Television? Say madly that we can have that as well.

Original walnut is carried indoors with awe and ceremony befitting sacred relic at least, and so strongly do I feel about Aga that I am almost surprised not to see it in kitchen when I go in.

Very nearly amidst all this excitement forget to tell Lee to ring Lady E-A, but I do remember, and he does, and they hold long conversation, result of which is that he commits us *both* to taking part in forthcoming production of highly melodramatic play, hitherto unknown to me. (Shall pretend I know it well.) Lee says that his part is that of young handsome foreign nobleman, with artistic and sensitive nature. What is mine? I ask. He replies that he thinks it is an elderly refugee charwoman. I am slightly indignant about this and ask who else is to be in it, but he does not know, except that Lady E-A is to take the title role, some Duchess or Empress or something. Can only hope they will all enjoy themselves, and go away to clean bathroom and get into the spirit of my part.

*Sunday, 30th*
Day devoted to entertaining London friends Janet and husband and children, playing return match after our recent visit to them. They arrive late for lunch which is a blessing, as I am as usual behind-hand with it, and all goes well. Janet

dressed in tremendous sheepskin jacket in which she looks well, though I shouldn't, and children Jeremy and Julian behave well and have great charm. Am forced to conclusion that both are definitely more intelligent than J and T, Jeremy kindly tells me how to make what he calls "nice cosy waffles" and Julian on request converses in fluent French. Have not even the consolation of thinking that they are older than J and T as both are younger, also better-looking and better dressed. Have made tremendous effort to supply notable lunch, with rather unworthy motive of going one better than Janet and her bohemianism when we went to her, but am foolish enough to leave trolley laden with stewed pears, cream and meringues where Ben can get at it while we are having sherry before lunch. He has splendid orgy and is found covered with cream and meringue and everyone is amused and indulgent but I am very cross and mess in dining-room and on trolley take ages to clear up. (Cream somehow covers wall, carpet and floor; am only surprised there is any left, and wallpaper will never be the same again.)

Lunch eventually very late indeed but successful except for slight shortage of meringues and lack of appetite on Ben's part. We all go round the garden afterwards and Janet and husband, like all town dwellers, know far more about gardening and Nature in general than we do and give us several useful tips, which we assure them we shall follow. (Lee, I observe, really intends to. Know well that that is as far as it will get.)

I say, Well what about a cup of tea, Janet says No no they must be getting back. I repeat that they must have a cup of tea (shall be done in the eye if they don't as I have made a cake specially), and they continue to say, but with less conviction, that they must be going. Wish I had put the kettle on before we started the argument, it would have been boiling by the time they decide that they *will* have just a quick cup. We all have a quick cup (and cake) and are just having it when there is ring at front door bell. I am startled and look round corner of window to see who it is as Lee goes to door. See old friends Robert and Anne, and give quick hissing biography of them to Janet; just as I am saying They have Two Little Boys Too, Lee ushers them into room preceded by three little girls. Am completely thrown out of gear by this and have great difficulty remembering anybody's name to perform introductions. Robert and Anne say they were just picnicking nearby and hope we don't mind, they have a few other children with them but don't think they have got any diseases. It eventually transpires that there are five children with them altogether, their own two quite submerged, and I am unable to sort any of them out and turn the whole lot into the garden with James, Toby, Jeremy, Julian and Ben. Lee produces sherry and we all talk about fabulous value of walnut trees, horrors of school fees (Lee and I preserve discreet silence about Great-Aunt Elizabeth), Cost of Living of which I am sick and tired, and film *Genevieve* which makes us all shriek with reminiscent laughter. Conversation interrupted by enormous seething mass of children who now descend on us, hitting each other freely, and all are taken away by their respective parents. Impossible not to reflect that there was something to be said for Nannies; have never, since attaining what is said to be Woman's Highest Sphere, succeeded in holding uninterrupted conversation with any other adult for more than five minutes, but try to console myself with reflection that at least it will be worse when they are older and can't be pushed off to bed; which I proceed to do.

Realise that I have unpleasantly sore throat as result of day's excitements and go to bed early.

# OCTOBER

*Monday, 1st*

Throat still very sore, complain bitterly about it but get no sympathy. Spend morning as usual doing beastly washing and housework and cooking, and deploring drudgery of housework. Gloom lifts however when I suddenly remember about walnut tree and I instantly ring up local timber merchant. Tell him that we have this tree and say, I hope nonchalantly, that We are Thinking of Selling it. He sounds interested and says How big is it? Have no idea, but say Oh quite large, very tall anyway. He says that it is the Diameter that Matters, and that he would like to come and see it. This afternoon? I ask, trying not to sound too excited, This afternoon, he promises.

Tell Ben all about the Aga we are going to have. Trappist child very useful repository for such confidences.

While he is having his rest read paper and am made very angry by letter from Unknown about Drudgery of Housewifery and deplorable fact that housewives have no leisure and wouldn't know how to use it if they had. Am inspired to pen angry reply saying that I am a housewife and that I have lots of leisure and that I use it with the utmost intelligence. Rush down the road and post it before I think better of it. Wonder afterwards if it was entirely accurate, in view of this mornings depression, but too late to recall now, and anyway paper never publishes my letters.

Timber merchant calls, very unattractive figure in dirty raincoat (why? very fine autumn day, hasn't he got a jacket?) and I hump Ben on my hip and escort him to walnut tree. He looks at it in silence for some time and I wonder how I am going to persuade him up to three hundred if he only offers two, and he then utters to the effect that It will be a very valuable tree in a Hundred Years Time. Bitterly disappointed, Aga, Bendix, new car, television set and all fly away in dissolving dream, but am determined to show no emotion and pretend to be unmoved. Last effort is to say Are there any other trees here he would be interested in as we are thinking of clearing quite a lot? He looks scornfully round and says He will clear the lot for me for Fifteen pounds if I like. Fifteen Pounds? I repeat astonished. It won't cost you more than

that, he asserts. I am speechless, had no intention of *me* paying *him* anything, indeed am in no position to. Usher him back to front gate. (Ben getting heavier and heavier but refuses to walk under own steam, just as well really as he is still incredibly slow and I want to get rid of timber merchant, throat getting sorer every minute and I am consumed with disappointment.) Timber merchant however refuses to go, and stays chatting on in most tiresome way, showing disgusting tendency to edge up closer and closer to me and eying me with nasty bleary eye in manner that I can only call *lecherous*. (Very unflattering, he is repellent in the extreme and I am looking rather fatter and more untidy than usual.) Finally get rid of him by saying Well I must Take the baby in, and walking away from him. Peep through dining-room window when inside to see if he really has gone and see him standing in road looking at dead laburnum tree in hedge. Only wish it would fall on him.

Throat too sore to speak, am thankful when Lee comes home early and hand children over to him and go to bed. He says Am I getting Tonsillitis? Yes I am.

*Tuesday, 2nd*
Am prostrate. Lee copes with everything, does breakfast and sends children off to school and arranges for Ben to go to Susan for day. Papers arrive and my letter *has* been printed, and am astonished and gratified, but wish I hadn't been quite so enthusiastic about joys of being single-handed housewife. Not joyful at all when incapacitated.

Susan rings up to ask How I am and to express

sympathy; thank her for looking after Ben and she says she is delighted as it will get her into practice. I say excitedly Then you really are going to have one? and she says Well yes it begins to look like it, but I'm not to tell anyone. She then says that she has read my letter in the paper (tone very disapproving, think she thinks I have gone too far this time), and that its All very well but what about this sort of thing? Agree that there are times when help in the house would be an advantage, and she makes long and kindly-intentioned speech about How the time has really come when she must tell me that she thinks I am Very Foolish, it is No Kindness to Anyone to try to do too much, and Very Unfair on Lee and the children. Long to make impassioned speech in my own defence but throat really too sore and anyway present situation hardly supports my case. She concludes giving me address of Agency through which I can obtain Foreign Help, for which I meekly thank her. Would like to point out that I cannot afford it, but she spikes my guns by adding that it need hardly cost anything as if I have a girl *au pair* I don't have to pay her any wages. This sounds very improbable to me and very unfair to girl concerned but have crossed swords with Susan before, she is always right about everything and anyway cannot be bothered to argue. Thank her again for having Ben, say I am feeling much better which is true, and ring off.

Would very much like a light invalidish lunch but as it would mean getting up to get it for myself do not bother. Hope starvation day will slim me.

Get up in time to welcome children back from school,

cook them large tea of bacon and eggs, but both say they have sore throats and refuse to eat. Realise they have got my germ and feel like a leper.

*Wednesday, 3rd*
James and Toby both in bed, tonsillitis, know exactly how they feel but nevertheless find it very difficult to be soothing and sympathetic. Spend day trying to keep Ben out of their room, reading to them at cost of distinct relapse in state of my own throat, (Just So stories great success but NOT Alice inWonderland), making them hot blackcurrant drinks and tidying up their room. (Why do all little boys' toys consist of infinitesimally small parts designed for getting lost in and under beds?)

Toby spends great part of the day singing hymns and I wonder if he is going to die.

Lee, on return from work, tells me that all his colleagues have read my letter in newspaper and are Mocking him about it. I am indignant and he explains that they assert that if his wife has so much leisure it must mean that he does all the housework. Had been just about to ask him to do the washing-up but refrain, decide instead to write to Agency and obtain foreign girl to come to us *au pair*.

Lee is sympathetic about tonsilitis but adds that He has been saying for ages that Those Children's Tonsils ought to be Looked At, and that he has made an appointment for us all to be seen by eminent local Ear Nose and Throat specialist. Wish Lee's position as embryo specialist in obscure branch of medicine did not mean that we can apparently never call on excellent local g.p. like anybody else.

*Monday, 8th*

Immense correspondence under way between self and German girl who asserts herself Willing to do Much Work for me, exchange of photographs is effected (German girl, Greta, very pretty; constant reading of inferior novels leads me to wonder if a touch of drama will be added to our lives in event of Lee being overwhelmed by her charms), and she assures me that she loves already my so charming family and repeats her desire to work for me with All her Might. Would find it very much easier to take her letters seriously if she did not interlard them so copiously with exclamation marks, and am disposed to scoff at this habit until Lee tells me that I am being Very Insular.

First rehearsal of Local Drama group takes place, very kindly arranged at our house to save us expense of baby-sitter. (Would be more grateful for this dispensation if it did not entail extra amount of housework to make sure that sitting-room is fit to be seen.) All wasted as Lady E-A plumps for Dining-room as being more suitable, where she shifts furniture around briskly, revealing squalid piles of dust, marbles and minibricks. Members of Drama Group arrive with varying degrees of punctuality and show tendency to huddle in corners with their coats on. Lady E-A exhibits brisk *bonhomie* and rallies us all rousingly, jollies us into position for Act One Scene One, and discovers that Leading Lady is absent. We all relax and show tendency to return to our corners like so many boxers. Elderly Lady, name unknown but very odd skirt, smiles charmingly at me and produces learned tome out of her pocket and settles down to some quiet study. Lee and the only other two men in cast (both young and good-looking, where on earth did Lady E-A find them?) discuss Damp Patch in corner behind toy-cupboard. Remaining members, females of uncertain age but skittish appearance, get out their knitting and discuss last year's Pantomime. Lady E-A braces us all up by saying Well well this won't do, we're just wasting these good people's time (looking dotingly at Lee as she says it). We won't wait for Fanny, I can't think what has happened to her she's always such a Good Trouper. She'll just have to take Fanny's part herself. This she proceeds to do, as rehearsal finally gets going; and am obliged to admit she does it very well. Have in fact to suppress unworthy thought that whole thing was a put-up job to give her a bit of fun.

Lee acquits himself well, though not in my opinion so brilliantly as to deserve eulogies that Lady E-A pours out on him. I, on the contrary, do less well, and have to be told three times to Speak Up. (Only have four things to say.) Explain that I am inhibited by knowledge that children are asleep immediately overhead and everyone assumes exaggeratedly contrite whispers for at least five minutes.

Leading Lady, Fanny, arrives just as we are finishing. Very startling apparition in tartan slacks and turban; looks and figure well able to take it, and very stagey manner which is attractive rather than the opposite. (Can see that Lee is looking disapproving though.) Lady E-A embraces her warmly and says Darling you naughty girl where have you been? Fanny quite unrepentant and embarks on long story about having been misinformed as to whereabouts of our house. (Great nonsense, village not as labyrinthine as all that and anyway everybody knows where everybody else lives.) Lady E-A becomes annoyed and interrupts frequently. Fanny waves her arms about and rolls her eyes and says Really we've No Idea . . . but Lady E-A drowns her with assertion that We'll never get anywhere if People can't arrive in time. Argument continues for a long time with more and more endearments and breathless attention from the rest of us, and concludes with Lady E-A offering to Resign and Fanny saying Darling don't be ridiculous, just tell me Where and When the next rehearsal is to be. Elderly skirt lady looks up from learned tome to which she has remained glued and says she thinks she'd better go home now because of Mother. Am astonished that she still has a mother. Other members mutter similar excuses and edge towards door. Make half-hearted offer of Cups of Tea, and Lady E-A says Oh no child you're not to feel you have to entertain us, she knows how difficult things are. Feel obliged after that to go and put the kettle on if only to prove that poverty is not yet so extreme as to prevent me buying tea, milk and sugar. Am reduced however to hovering in kitchen until I hear at least two people leave as have not enough cups to go round, and as it is have to drink own tea out of Ben's mug. Last members finally leave at midnight with unconvincing promises that We will all know Act One by next time.

*Tuesday, 9th*
Visit to Ear Nose and Throat specialist takes place. Very singular experience. Specialist is enormous man like Robert Mitchum only jovial, is nice to the boys and peers down

their throats and says they Look Very Healthy. Am rather annoyed by this as had hoped that he would offer to remove their tonsils instantly and that thereby neither would ever be ill again. Say as much, more or less, whilst removing Ben from expensive and dangerous looking machine in the corner, and R. Mitchum says pityingly that Mothers always seem to think that. Do not like implication that all mothers are stupid and me with them, but before I can rally he adds that While I'm here he'd better have a Look at Me Too. Children are removed by a secretary, wish her joy of them, and I am Looked at. R. Mitchum becomes excited and says Ah yes, just as he thought, there are Remnants here. Say, with difficulty owing to practically dislocated jaw, that I had my tonsils out in early childhood. Yes yes, says R. Mitchum, he thought as much, in *those* days . . . and pursues his researches painfully into my gullet. Do not at all care for being relegated to antiquity. He shakes his head and says he doesn't at all like to think what may be going on under that scar tissue. Nor do I. Further indignities ensue as he investigates my nose, only breaking off to say Is that a Family Beak or did I Break it some time? Final horror reached when he announces that He'd like to have those Remnants Out. I revert feebly to the children and offer him their tonsils and adenoids too if he likes, instead? He brushes this aside and says when could I manage it? It would mean a Week in Hospital and then *at least* a week's convalescence. Lack the moral courage to say what I really think which is No thank you not now or *ever*, and say instead that I will Have to Work things Out. Make mental resolve never to go near him again, and hurry away with many expressions of gratitude. Do not really feel he is deceived for one moment, but realise later that maybe this is his formula for getting rid of tiresome mothers? Rather ingenious if so.

Give children fish and chips at sordid café which they appear to regard as last word in sophistication, Ben shows off and collects indulgent glances which become noticeably less as meal continues, and cease entirely long before we finally pay bill and leave.

James asks anxiously whether we have enough petrol to get home, I tell him rather sharply to Mind his own business, and Toby leans lovingly on large Bentley that is parked next to us in car park and says That is the sort of car he will have when he is grown-up. Detach him before rightful owner returns as he is making sticky finger-marks on windows, and James says he won't be able to afford one like that if he's going into the Navy. Toby replies that Yes he will because he's not going to have a Wife. Run out of petrol on the way home.

Second post awaiting us when we finally get home brings two letters from Germany, again stiff with exclamation marks, giving two totally contradictory schedules of Greta's proposed journey to England. Post marks blurred and Greta's writing of date sufficiently confusing to give me no clue as to which letter cancels out which. Both letters however full once again of encouraging sentiments as to her willingness to do All that I shall wish her to do for the Herr Doktor! and the Lovely boys! dear Madam! Toby disconcerts me frightfully by asking casually Whether this girl knows he's the Bad One? Wonder if I ought to send him to a psychiatrist? Or me?

Mrs Parnell says over the fence that she hears I've Been Poorly, if only she'd known she'd have Brought me in Something and What was the trouble? Tell her as briefly as possible but am unable to stem flood of reminiscence about her own family's throat troubles, which have apparently all been far worse than ours, and that she for her part is Never Free from it. Refrain from retorting that in that case I wish she would keep her germs to herself.

*Wednesday, 10th*
Entire day spent in fever of preparation for having Lee's new chief and wife to dinner. Both unknown to me and feel that it is imperative that good impression should be made. Have procured ancient Boiling Fowl and propose to do it in pressure cooker in order to de-toughen it before making *fricassée* which is my only party piece. Chicken is too large to fit in pressure cooker. Am in despair until milkman arrives, confide my troubles to him and he is amused but consoling, says that A Bit of Strength is all that's needed, and bravely reduces the fowl to manageable proportions with his bare hands. (Hope they are reasonably clean.) He then points out that a Drop of Cream will make All the Difference to *the fricassée*, and I can do no less than immediately buy some from him.

Shortly after he has left frightful screams emerge from the playroom and Ben appears, covered in blood, having cut his hand to the bone on broken fire-engine of James'. Urgent medical attention obviously necessary, cannot think what to do, wrap injured hand up in kitchen towel and dash out into road to see if milkman is still in sight.

He is not, but unknown woman is walking past, looks kind, and I say desperately Can she come in a minute? She rallies round nobly and holds the still-bellowing Ben while I get car out and we drive to the g.p.'s surgery. Other patients, who have presumably been waiting hours, are kind and sympathetic and let us go in next. G.P. is also kind but points out that This is a Nasty Cut, which I can see for myself, and we had better go straight into Casualty and have it Sewn Up. Kind unknown woman says she will come with us (am worried about what she was really on her way to do, but she brushes her own affairs aside in the most noble way), and we drive twelve miles to Hospital. Ben is removed to be dealt with, unknown Good Samaritan and I sit in Outpatients and wait. Presently she says she feels sick and disappears. I become aware that I too feel sick, and am moreover trembling violently. Also realise that I am still dressed in remarkably grubby sweater and slacks which have defective zip. Other outpatients show tendency to edge nervously away from me. At this point Lee arrives from department of Hospital where he works and I feel better, though slightly ashamed of appearance, and my stock obviously goes up with other outpatients. Shortly after this Ben is restored to us, heavily bandaged and with nine stitches in hand, but otherwise restored to normality. Good Samaritan is found pacing the grounds and we drive home again. Good Samaritan tells me where to drop her and vanishes before I can thank her at all adequately for her kindness. Return home feeling hundreds of years older and very disinclined to cope with further plans for dinner tonight. Ben however is unmoved by his experiences, and appears not to notice that one hand is out of action, so I endeavour to pull myself together and return to chicken; pressure cooker has been cooking away all this time, at least it should be tender.

Day continues curiously disorganised but manage to get children off to bed before scheduled time of arrival of Lee's chief, Professor Henning. Get self ready (red corduroy skirt nice but too tight round waist, must not breathe deeply. Nylon blouse also nice, I think, but of course transparent, and wonder if Mrs H will recognise that undergarment clearly to be seen through it comes from cheap chain store? Console myself by reflecting that if she *does* recognise it it will mean she goes there herself.)

Go and do last-minute fiddlings-about in kitchen, add milkman's cream madly to everything, and spill quite large dollop of tomato soup on skirt. Thank goodness skirt is red.

Lee rings up three minutes before Professor is due and says he's frightfully sorry he's going to be late. I curse him freely. He repeats that he is frightfully sorry, he'll come as soon as he can, and how is Ben? Peacefully asleep, I say optimistically, but for Heaven's sake hurry up and come home, and even as I say it can hear sound of car turning in at gateway. Ring off and have another quick dab at stain on skirt before welcoming guests with (I hope) air of charming and gracious hostess.

Professor turns out to be tiny little man with sleepy expression exactly like the Dormouse in Alice, makes me feel like an Amazon, but wife, I am uncharitably delighted to see, is definitely fat. Both however are charming and I ply them with sherry and cigarettes and make conscientious efforts to do Lee credit and talk about Cultured Matters. Rather hampered in this by gradually growing conviction that Ben has been woken up by their arrival and is roaring. Listen for this with one ear and to Professor's dissertation on the hospitality he received on recent American Lecture Tour (bet it was better than what I am offering this evening) with the other. We then get on to Gardening, Mrs Professor evidently an expert (thank goodness it is dark) at which point Lee dashes in full of apologies. Ben's crying by this time distinctly audible to everyone and am at last able to relinquish cares of hospitality and go to comfort him which I have been dying to do all along. Give Lee a sharp look as I go which I hope he understands means I am furious with him for being late, that he is to do something about his hair which is all standing on end, and that he is not to talk shop with the Dormouse. Very difficult to get all that into one look.

Minister to Ben.

While I am occupied with him hear fearful sounds of battle from James and Toby's room and unmistakable sound of one of them going downstairs. Am furious but helpless. Subsequently learn from Lee that this is James, nose bleeding profusely, Toby having woken and on sudden ungodly impulse hit his sleeping brother in the face. All hopes of gracious social evening and good impression at an end, but Dormouse is magnificent and he and wife rally round and with Lee restore peace.

Finally have dinner very late indeed but by this time feel we all know one another very well indeed.

After they have left Lee says he begins to see why I want Greta.

*Thursday, 11th*

Charming American, recently met at cocktail party, rings up to say Its very short notice but she is giving small birthday party for Junior who is Ben's age and would Ben care to come along? Make rapid mental plans to send James and Toby to Susan on return from school, and accept.

J and T are offended at not being included but agree to go and watch Television at Susan's and Ben and I set out. Quite incredible scene of confusion greets us at birthday party. Charming American is exactly like something out of *Gone With the Wind*, beautifully dressed and made-up but clasping a shrieking baby and in despair because she Seems to be Kinda Disorganised. Nothing is ready for the party. Charming American, name is Maybelle, says she has Sent Cliff round to the store for a Few Things but she can't think what's keeping him. "Few Things" apparently include all food for the party except what she refers to as Candy and Cookies, which she proceeds to ask me very nicely to arrange on the table for her. By this time am already holding the still-shrieking baby but do my best. Another mother is called into service to blow up balloons. Maybelle says again that she can't think what's keeping Cliff, and spills a bottle of orange squash all over the floor. Another mother mops it up.

Cliff finally lopes in laden with food, and is despatched to change and feed the baby. He obeys without a murmur (can feel all the English mothers making a mental note of this phenomenon). Table is finally declared ready, children, who have been under supervision of only remaining mother, are summoned and sat down at table. Maybelle clasps her hands and says Well Gee, kids, isn't this a swell party? and My, Junior, aren't you having *fun*? and continues to make these and similar exclamations. (Had hitherto supposed that people only talked like this in films.) The rest of us pour drinks, pass sandwiches and pick up crumbs. Children, average age about three, are stolid but eat chocolate biscuits, and Ben gains considerable prestige with his bandaged hand. He becomes obstreperous and obtains further attention by dipping his bandage in his drink and sucking it; other mothers laugh indulgently and Maybelle rolls her eyes affectedly. Busy myself with another child and pretend not to see. Cake candles are lit and Maybelle makes us all sing Happy Birthday To You; children remain silent but grown-ups do their best, in appallingly high key set by Maybelle, and such is the force of her personality that I suddenly become aware that we are all singing with strong American accents. Junior (nose needs wiping) blows candles out after several efforts and children are all given cake, which none of them eat.

Maybelle suddenly throws us all into confusion by screeching that Oh her *goodness* she meant just to put up some snacks for the grownups, how *awful*, and we are all pressed into service grilling things on toast. She adds doubtfully that she guesses we'd all like tea too? and that she just can't make tea right for you English. We make tea and carry trays off to the drawing-room. Maybelle follows us and becomes exclusively occupied with Cliff and various other fathers who have by now arrived. Children are left with remains of tea. Feel it necessary to hurry back to see if they are all right, which they are, having all got down and settled to their own pursuits on the floor. Feel that while I am there I might as well stoke up the boiler which is nearly out and is, I feel, unlikely to be dealt with by Maybelle. Am joined by another mother who has come down to do the washing-up. I help her and we do not say anything about our hostess.

Finally take my departure, with Ben, feeling completely exhausted. Maybelle waves us off with much gaiety, still looking as fresh as a daisy. Reflect that the really extraordinary thing is that despite everything I still am completely under the spell of her charm. Only wish that I could get away with the same sort of thing, but am only too well aware that you have to have the right build to get away with the Helpless Little Woman act.

*Friday, 12th*

Cheque arrives from *Daily Tabard*. Still no sign of article appearing in print but am far too delighted with cheque to care. Resolve to buy a new dress.

Lee on being told of this intention says Well of course it's my money, it's up to me, but he's just got the bill from the garage for last repairs done to my car and it's precisely Fifteen Guineas. Hand cheque over to him in disgust and relinquish dreams of new dress. (Ought to slim before buying new clothes anyway.)

Further shock administered by documents in letter from prep school including list of clothes that James will require there. Had always thought my children were quite adequately dressed but was evidently wrong as he will have to have every single thing new. Entire outfit looks as though it will cost as much as one term's fees, and why "two pairs stockings if trousers worn only on Sundays"? Do not understand this at all.

Greta due to arrive tomorrow, spend much time arranging her room. Have promised "own bed-sitting room" and have much difficulty carting large dilapidated armchair upstairs to fulfil this. Room still looks uncompromisingly "bed", sacrifice small card-table and stand it in front of window so that she can write letters. Put little embroidered

cloth on it diagonally, think that this looks suburban and take it off again, but surface of table not improved by torn baize and inkstains and decide that Germans *like* things to be suburban and put it on again. Bulb missing from bedside lamp (why, it was there when Hermione came to stay, did she take it away with her?), must remember to get one. (Other housewives always have a neat pile of spare bulbs in store cupboard. Why can't I housekeep properly? Refuse to believe that I am totally incompetent but difficult at present to see the slightest justification for this claim.)

James on return from school offers to polish the furniture and I let him, and he spills all the polish on the carpet, and is hurt when I am not pleased. Fundamental difference of opinion here between me and all my family, they maintaining that good intentions are what count, while I hold that Actions Speak Louder etc; however argument on the subject gets us nowhere and I work off my feelings mopping up polish which has made indelible stain on carpet.

Some woman on the wireless the other day said that scrubbing and polishing floors had kept her waistline neat, mine ought to rival any wasp soon.

*Saturday, 13th*
*Daily Tabard* reported by B.B.C. to be on verge of bankruptcy. Not surprised.

Lee goes off to London to meet Greta. Takes James with him but not Toby who has tendency to be car-sick. Toby complains bitterly over injustice of this and I waste much time trying to explain, but all as usual ends in undignified shouting match, and Toby departs to garden looking injured.

Lee returns much later than expected, obviously ex-hausted; Greta emerges from car, not a bit like photographs, tall and pale and evidently highly emotional. Seizes me by both hands and makes long passionate speech in German. Cannot understand a word except Ach Gott several times. Withdraw hands kindly and make slightly less passionate speech in English saying how Delighted I am to see her and that I hope she will feel at Home with us. She shakes her head madly (marmalade profusion of curls wag all over the place), rolls her eyes and says Yes, Yes, So Kind, but all other English words evidently elude her. Take her up to her room, she clasps her hands and gazes about her with many Teutonic exclamations and becomes tearful. I leave her to settle herself in with what I think kind tact, but fear she may interpret as British callousness.

Lee says curtly Well now I've got her he hopes I like her. Realise with horror he has taken against her. Say hopefully She seems nice don't you think? Lee says shortly that she was Sick in the Car Twice, and seems to think I should be sorrier for him than her on this account. Overhear James telling Toby in the playroom that Greta *Kissed* Him, feel sorrier than ever for the poor girl, it will take her weeks to live that down. Take her a cup of tea, fear the Britishness of this may finish her off entirely, but it is well received and am thankful to find that her knowledge of English has returned to her. We converse amiably, she assures me that House and Children are Charming (says nothing about Lee, hope he wasn't absolutely beastly to her), and refuses my offer that she should Lie Down on her Bed.

Spend rest of day making friends with Greta and

showing her round house and garden. Decide that she is a nice girl full of willingness and feel full of hope that emotional hand-wavings, shruggings and exclamations will die away when she feels More Settled. (Very unlike preconceived idea of German *fräulein.*) Thrust Ben at her at every possible opportunity as Lee and James and Toby are behaving in most infuriating fashion and keeping as far away from us as they can. This unfair in almost every direction as Lee is Setting the Boys a Bad Example and is moreover the only one in the family who knows any German. Shall have a lot to say to him in bed tonight.

Take early opportunity to work on James' kind heart about being Nice to Foreign Girl in Strange Land, and he is co-operative and later gives her a toffee, keeping pointedly at arms' length as he does so. Toby avoids any *tête-à-tête* with me, shall simply content myself as far as he is concerned with trying to prevent him from actually biting the poor girl.

Force Lee, later in evening after children are in bed, to speak German, which after an uncertain start he does with increasing skill and fluency. Whole conversation is Greek to me but Greta is animated and I feel that atmosphere of friendliness has been generated which seems promising.

*Monday, 15th*
Greta now quite established as one of the family. Is producing several very irritating tricks which I resolve not to be annoyed by. Cannot, for instance, see that it is necessary to keep bedroom window hermetically sealed and electric heater full on all the time, particularly when she uses so

much strong scent. Tell myself that if this is what makes a homelike atmosphere for her I must not interfere, can always air the room when she goes out and must never let Lee know about the heater. Wish also that she would not spring to her feet with clasped hands and a glad cry whenever I ask her to do anything as it throws me off my balance to such an extent that I can never remember what I was going to say. Wish also that she would not *moo* over Ben so sentimentally. Resolutions of not getting irritated obviously in grave danger of breaking down, wish I had more control over my own mental processes.

Ring up Susan and tell her, as much for own benefit as hers, that Greta is unqualified success. Susan has no scruples about saying She Told me so several times, and adds Now perhaps I'll do something about my Appearance? Would like to be offended but know all too well that she is fully justified, present state of figure, hair and clothes entirely deplorable. Confess this meekly and Susan is managing but kind and recommends instant visit to ducal establishment in London where she goes for her hair. She will fix up an appointment for me she says, with her Mr Charles, and after that I am to go to Harrods and buy a new hat. Jib at this so firmly that she relents and lets me off the hat, but hair appointment is agreed upon and I leave it all in her hands.

Greta cooks lunch and appears at ten to one, making extraordinary little curtsy like a convent-child which I try not to be astonished at, saying All is Not Quite ready, but Soon, Please? and Shall she Ring? (Sausages and mash clearly being given unprecedentedly meticulous care.) Say

Yes yes, any time, and find myself in unnatural state of having Nothing to Do for next few minutes. Am quite bewildered. Decide to be a Real Lady and sit in sitting-room with newspaper before lunch, cannot quite rise to solitary glass of sherry but smoke cigarette and feel dashing. Newspaper very boring. Greta rings enormous cow-bell, kept by back door for purpose of summoning Lee to telephone from far end of garden, am startled and deafened but try to make reasonable show of sailing regally in to lunch. Sausage and mash in kitchen perhaps something of an anti-climax. Must consider using the dining-room again now that we have Greta, can it be that Gracious Living is just around the corner?

*Friday, 19th*
Go to London. Hardly credible, have not been anywhere without children for years and years, feel very odd. Curious how much more time there is, catch London train quite easily and spend journey relishing pleasure of being allowed to read magazine uninterruptedly. Feel sophisticated. On arrival in London however note with dismay that appearance has deteriorated sharply since last sight of it in mirror at home, best coat and skirt definitely baggy and stain on lapel *does* show, shoes gape in a way reminiscent of Minnie Mouse and hairdresser will probably refuse to admit me. Wish I had worn a hat but this waste of time and must concentrate on not getting run over and on finding way to highpowered hairdressing establishment recommended by Susan.

Buses and Underground as usual confuse me to such an

extent that have eventually to get taxi. Ask taxi-driver for *Cecile* of Grafton St., he tells me firmly that what I mean is *Cecile* of Bruton St., agree that he is probably right, and we shortly arrive at ducal establishment. Uniformed commissionaire springs forward but at sight of me apparently changes his mind and springs away again, and am rather offended though relieved at not having to tip him. Wonder uneasily however whether he thought I looked mean, or poverty-stricken. Probably both.

Enter ducal establishment and am faced with enormous flight of marble stairs exactly like a pantomime, littered with scornful lacquered ladies whom I am much too frightened of to ask the way. They all look at me and I hurry upstairs, effect marred by one shoe coming off. Arrive eventually at the top and am rescued by compassionate lady with purple hair who disconcerts me all over again by snatching my coat from me, fact that I am wearing wide white elastic belt to keep skirt up is hideously revealed and am thankful when she proceeds to drape me in pink nylon smock. Out she then leads me to enormous hall full of clients being *done*, dressing tables, driers, film-star like assistants and quantities of gilt cupids.

Mr Charles, recommended by Susan, appears and seats me in front of a dressing-table and we both look gloomily at my reflection. He fingers my hair distastefully and sends for film-star to wash it. (Washed it myself yesterday, rather hurt.) Film star drapes me backwards over a basin from which peculiar position I am able to study remarkable *bas-relief* on ceiling; large apocryphal figure with minions and clouds; (God and the angels? Satan and Co? Mr Charles

71

and filmstars?) Clean and dripping I am returned to Mr Charles. Start to tell him what I want; cut so that it goes into waves, please, like Mrs Evershed's. Mrs Evershed? says Mr C. Would that be Mrs Evershed from Surrey? No, I say, apologetically, the one from Berks. Oh *Berks*, says Mr C disappointedly. Evidently not a very reputable county. He relapses into silence and cuts my dripping hair with considerable venom and without apparently ever looking at it. Am horrified and force myself to stop looking. Am anyway distracted by sight of unusually glamorous customer returning from wash-basins whose back-view reveals interesting fact, through gap in maternity smock, that she is only wearing a brassiere. My eyes pop nearly out of my head; no petticoat, this is Life.

Mr C finally finishes snipping and pinning and parks me under drier in blissfully comfortable armchair. Very nearly go to sleep but feel that this would not be sophisticated thing to do, am bored by fashion magazine supplied and look instead at my neighbour under next drier. Am very impressed by her as she is strong-mindedly doing her own nails, with polish that I note is made by rival firm. Wonder she hasn't been asked to leave.

Final appearance when dry and unpinned staggers me; hair undoubtedly waving, whole face looks much better shape than usual and am very pleased, though less so when I am allowed to see back and observe that Mr C has seen fit to sweep it all sideways. Ask nervously if he thinks I'll be able to manage that myself at home? He is astonished and says But *yes*, this is how the hair *wants* to go. So that's what's been wrong with it all these years. Moral uplift is complete and I pay enormous bill without (I hope) blenching and sweep down pantomime stairs internally making rude gestures at lacquered ladies. (See, I'm just as glamorous as you now.)

Must cash in on this unaccustomed feeling of superiority, realise that I am not impossibly far from office of distinguished publisher known to me in early childhood, and take unprecedented step of going to visit him.

Distinguished publisher is in, and am ushered instantly to his presence. He greets me kindly, and I wonder why on earth I have come. Try to buoy up my morale by remembering beauty of newly done hair, and wonder if publisher thinks it looks nice. Wonder if he thinks I always look like this. Ghastly thought, shall I have to go and have it done by Mr Charles every time I come and see publisher? But if I go to see publisher often implication is that I must be successful writer and therefore shall be able to afford Mr Charles as often as I like . . . rather involved daydream interrupted here by publisher who is, I suddenly realise, saying kindly that he supposes I have written a book? Seems so matter-of-fact about whole idea that I hardly dare admit that I have in fact only written part of one, and try to imply light-heartedly that I have tossed off a little masterpiece that is all but finished. Publisher (looks exactly like Demon King in pantomime, remember irrelevantly but vividly that I used to be madly in love with him when I was ten, he was at the top of my Marrying List for a long time) asks with utmost benevolence What book is about? Entirely reasonable question which I am unfortunately unable to answer, as have been relying heavily on Anthony Trollope's dictum that It is not necessary to know what is going to happen to one's characters, they will work themselves out. Do not feel up to explaining this. Mutter incomprehensibly until Demon King takes pity and interrupts by asking Whether book is to be illustrated and if so by whom? Suggest madly only artist's name I can think of, and add hopefully that he is so good at drawing children. Demon King looks aghast and says Not too much about children, he hopes? Mentally rewrite Chapter One and say No no, hardly at all. (Wish I knew what it *was* going to be about.) Demon King however is kindness itself and is encouraging about entire nebulous project and says he will Look forward to seeing manuscript. Am inspired to say idiotically that He won't accept it just out of kindness will he? Demon King is nicer about this than I deserve and asks after children. Make short speech about them but evidently not short enough as he expresses surprise that I have so many. Have evidently given impression of having huge seething litter. Say that it is not so much that there are many but that they cost so much to educate. (Reproachful shade of Great-Aunt Elizabeth hovers above me but I ignore it, feeling that Demon King must at all costs be brought to realise my extreme poverty.) Demon King however looks bland and takes wind out of my sails by saying But State Education is free now isn't it? Feel convicted of having been pretentious, am quite unable at this stage to embark on argument on pros and cons of Eleven-plus exam (of which I feel fairly sure Demon King has never heard), and take my leave.

Once out in the street cannot think what came over me at all ever to embark on entire enterprise, feel utterly alien, provincial and foolish and decide that the sooner I am back at the kitchen sink the better.

*Saturday, 20th*
Hair looks terrible after being slept on. Mrs Parnell takes one look at me over the fence and asks Where I had it Cut? In London, I say curtly. She replies without a vestige of expression Oh, and no more. Confirms my own impression that entire expedition yesterday was great waste of time and money.

Indoors find Greta enthusiastically cleaning sitting-room walls with floor-mop. Am delighted to find any house-work being done by anyone other than myself but cannot feel that this is a good idea, and tell her so, I hope kindly. She replies that Toby has tell her This is what Mop is For, and triumphantly harpoons disgusting cobweb from picture-rail. Enormous spider scuttles out from it and we shriek in unison and make concerted rush for hall. Feel that this slightly shaming accident has made us firm friends and wonder if modern Aesop's fable could not be evolved from it? Or perhaps introduction of spider into United Nations might be beneficial? For the present however content myself with telling her that Toby's advice is under all cir-cumstances to be regarded as highly suspect, and leave her to do vegetables for lunch while I go shopping.

Sole village grocer is, as usual on Saturday mornings, hub of local social world. Susan is there in deep conversa-tion with Lady E-A, both dressed apparently by Dior. They greet me with slightly patronising kindness and say nothing about my hair, nor indeed about the rest of my appearance which is perhaps as well. They ask about Greta. A great success, I assure them, and tell them about incident of mop, cobweb and spider. Story falls flat as both shudder affectedly at mention of cobweb, obviously no spider dares show its face in their highly organised households. Susan says Do I know that Lady E-A also has German girl (why? she has house full of minions), to whom she gives English lessons? Would Greta like to join in? Yes, I think she would. Lady E-A says It might be possible, but What *Class* is mine? Question fills me with fury, but can think of no reply which will both satisfy Lady E-A and placate grocer who is looking offended, as well he may. Lady E-A continues proudly that *hers* is Very Aristocratic, Somebody Von Something, and one has to be so careful doesn't one? Say as diplomatically as possible that I'm sure Greta will fit in very well with anyone (diplomacy rather marred by conviction that my face has gone bright scarlet with suppressed rage), and we agree to arrange English lessons in this high-class *ménage* if Greta thinks she can rise to it. Lady E-A then sails out and Susan buys all the most expensive things she can see in shop. Do I ever try this deep-frozen chicken, she asks? It's really very good and does nicely when there are only a few of you. Question not worth answering.

Do my own shopping in due course with usual depressing accompaniment of remarks like The Cheapest Sort you Have, please, and No, the *Small* packet please. Grocer suddenly produces from under the counter bottle of anaemic-looking liquid which he says is a new thing, pure lemon juice, very good for the complexion. Ask him, intending mild pleasantry, Why he should think I need it?

Grocer is covered with confusion and looks as though he is going to cry. Feel he has had an awful morning and order large bottle to cheer him up. Cannot imagine who will ever drink it. However scrutiny of label reveals that it is supposed to be slimming, so perhaps it will have its uses.

*Sunday, 21st*
Visit of Grandpapa. He has as usual refused to be fetched by car from nearby town where he lives, on grounds that this will give too much trouble to everyone, and arrives instead by one o'clock bus at neighbouring village. Wholly inconvenient for everyone including himself, but intentions good. Over lunch he tells me about old friend whose son has just become engaged. Grandpapa gloomy in the extreme about wisdom of this, and wants to know how I

think he should tell old friend that he doesn't care for son's fiancée? Ask if it wouldn't be simpler to say nothing at all? but Grandpapa shakes his head over this and says No, no, he feels he must just drop a tactful hint, perhaps it would do if he said he thought the boy was making a Great Mistake? Can only reflect that Grandpapa's ideas of tact and mine are never likely to coincide. Lunch otherwise great success, children behave rather better than usual as their grandfather, perhaps wisely, attempts no conversation with them, and fails to hear most of what they say.

He retires to sitting-room later with coffee and daily paper, has providently brought *The Times* with him, knowing all too well that we are not Top People, and goes to sleep.

Do washing-up with Greta, who says she *would* like to do English lessons with Lady E-A and her German girl. She is, she says, having Trouble to understand the Speeches of Shakespeare. (Can quite sympathise.) Could I for instance tell her in the English of today this speech of Hamlet of *To Be or Not to Be*? No I could not. Had no idea she had such cultured leanings, shall certainly send her off to Lady E-A and the aristocrat at the earliest possible opportunity.

Spend remainder of afternoon making tour of garden with Grandpapa and Lee. Grandpapa has much to say about apple trees, and points out many unusual features about them: American Blight here, canker there, this one is dead and that one ought to have been pruned properly years ago. Lee takes it all in and looks depressed, but Grandpapa becomes increasingly more and more cheerful and finally says that Upon his word he's never seen American Blight as widespread as this. Seems delighted about it and assures us that we'll Never Get Rid of it. Toby causes diversion at this point by walking on rather weedy flower-bed and is told by Grandpapa very briskly indeed to Get Off That *At Once*. (Bullying tones that all my little books on Parentcraft are united in agreeing should never be used when correcting sensitive growing boys.) To my unbounded astonishment Toby obeys instantly without a word of argument, not even a mutter or a scowl, and I later overhear him confiding to James that he Doesn't advise him to try to get away with much with Grandpapa, he's tried it and it doesn't work. (Food for considerable thought here, and perhaps article on Good Old-fashioned Discipline?)

Before leaving, Grandpapa assures me that I have Three Fine Boys, but evidently feels that they are rather too much in evidence as he goes on to tell me all about a splendid device called a *play-pen* which is used with much success by a young friend of his. Assure him that play-pens have been a great feature of our lives in the past but that even Ben is too big for one now, but Grandpapa is far too engrossed in subject to pay any heed to this and goes on to tell me more about play-pens and their advantages, and winds up really eloquent speech by saying that he thinks they were invented quite a long time ago and Was I ever put in one myself in early childhood? Lee says afterwards that he can't imagine anything more blissful than to be a father who doesn't even know whether or not his own child has a play-pen, and we ponder the joys of a bygone age whilst putting children to bed.

*Monday, 22nd*

Busy day, loomed over horribly by prospect of Hospital Dance in evening. Seem to be fatter than ever, can see no chance of getting into one and only evening-dress, and hair looks terrible. Defy Mr Charles and his sideswept nonsense and attack it with bacon scissors before washing it. Greta weeps over letter from Germany but assures me that this is Joy Only, she has hear from her Fiancé, and Ben says bad word beginning with "B" quite distinctly. Wish he would stay Trappist if that is best he can do.

Take James and Toby to dentist in afternoon. New dentist, both boys thoroughly due for check-up and both work themselves into hysterical frenzy on way there. I am brisk and bracing and assure them that this dentist is Very Gentle, and launch out on old familiar routine about advantages of Cleaning Teeth Thoroughly and how it's better to have Check-up Now than Trouble Later. Boys are unconvinced and James says bitterly that its All Very Well for me, I'm not going to be Tortured. Toby says Well *he* shouldn't have to have anything done, as he's been cleaning his teeth like anything lately. Point out that practice of eating toothpaste does not constitute proper dental hygiene, and he is offended and says he feels sick.

Dentist proves to be very tall man with hair like Beethoven; am delighted about height as this will give boys an opportunity for savouring to the full joys of being raised to skies in Chair. (Also, more selfishly, because any encounter with really tall man gives me unaccustomed sensation of *petite* femininity.) Less pleased about musician-like hair but perhaps this is a sign of genius. At all events he removes Toby, and James and I sit in very very contemporary waiting-room and he kicks furniture while I tell him not to. Can hear Toby's voice continuing uninterruptedly from dentist's room, cannot imagine how he manages to talk under such conditions or how dentist will achieve any of his researches, but evidently all is successful as Toby returns to us very shortly saying that Nothing Needed Doing. (Suppose that nothing could be seen past that wagging tongue.) James goes in and Toby and I look at *Punch*. Spend a long time trying to explain jokes to him with no success at all, but he concedes eventually that some of the advertisements are Quite Funny. Dead silence from dentist's room fills me with dismay. Eventually James returns, looking shifty, and Beethoven summons me out of earshot to ask Whether the Older Boy has always been of a Nervous Temperament? Refute this indignantly and then wonder if this is letting James down and add Well yes perhaps a bit. (What on earth can J have been doing?) Beethoven goes on to tell me in highly technical language all that needs doing to James' teeth and how he will need two more appointments *at least*, and Would I care to give him a Tranquilliser before the next time? Am deeply shocked both by suggestion and implication that James has been making such a to-do, and we part. In car going home James is ebullient and tells Toby that it's easy to get out of the dentist *doing* anything, all you have to do is to say *Ow* when he comes anywhere near you. Make long speech about British traditions of bravery and self-control which cuts no ice at all. Do not really know at this stage whether The Perfect Mother should be bracing or sympathetic, management of my children is as usual beyond me, shall leave it all to Beethoven in future.

Find Lee has got home before us, and that Greta has got tea ready. Blissful and unaccustomed state of affairs (but gravy-jug for milk *not* intelligent). Make customary feebly humorous enquiry as to whether there have been any Fascinating Telephone Calls during my absence? Lee replies dramatically Yes, the B.B.C. rang up. Beg him not to be funny. He says Honestly, he's not joking, they *did*. Miss Something or Other from Woman's Hour, and I am to ring back. Presence of children prevents me from telling him exactly how un-funny I think he is being, content myself with short unamused laugh and concentrate on tea. Lee says All right don't believe it if you don't want to but here is the number. By this time everyone else is fully convinced and screaming with excitement, Toby asking idiotically whether I shall be Reading the News and James saying No of course not it'll be Listen With Mother. Greta clasps hands and looks at me glowingly with many cries of Ach Gott. Ben proffers half-eaten chocolate biscuit. Lee tells me all over again that It is True, and finally come off churlish high-horse and become as excited as anyone.

All right I Will ring them up; what is this number? Lee gives it to me saying This is the Extension number and I am to ask for someone called Miss Affidavit or Addlepate or something like that. Very tiresome of him, cannot possibly ask for anything so idiotic, standard of elocution at B.B.C. must be surprisingly low or else his hearing needs attention. Ring number which is fortunately answered by cultured voice which says it is Miss Appleyard. (Perfectly easy to hear, always thought dear Lee was a bit deaf, he never hears half I say.) Miss A tells me at great length that she is delighted with Script which I have submitted (submission took place nearly a year ago, had forgotten all about it, she has been controlling her delight remarkably well), and will I come up for a Voice Test some time next week? Date is arranged, ring off full of joy, all is *couleur de rose*, now I am really going to be Famous. Am brought back to reality very sharply by Lee who asks whether I have pressed his dinner-jacket, and by James and Toby who are hitting each other.

Get ready for Dance. Am sufficiently elated by B.B.C.'s belated recognition of my talents to relapse into daydream in bath; broadcast . . . success . . . further broadcasts . . . nation-wide popularity . . . panellist on Television . . . (with usual hasty proviso that I shall be slim and *soignée* by then), and am just evolving rather witty little speech to be given by me at Prize-giving at my old school (Our Distinguished Old Girl) when James comes in looking agitated and says He doesn't like to Tell Tales but Toby has kicked Greta and Greta is crying. Spend much time dashing about in dressing-gown trying to restore peace, and resign witty speech at Old School to limbo. Struggle into evening-dress, do face and hair and decide conceitedly that I look nice. Am just practising charming smiles in front of looking-glass when Lee appears looking heated and saying he Can't find his dress-shirt, last worn a year ago for a Dinner. Search madly in bathroom which is where his clothes live in frightful confusion amongst boys' outgrown things, due to lack of space in bedroom. No sign of shirt. He becomes indignant and says It's a pity I can't look after his clothes properly. Knowledge that he is entirely justified annoys me intensely and we bicker unavailingly as we continue to search. Point of divorce practically reached when I discover shirt scrumpled up in polythene bag at bottom of wardrobe. Remember distinctly that I alone am responsible for this, had intended to send it to Chinese laundry but forgot all about it; feel very contrite but have long passed stage of being able to admit this, can only endeavour to make amends by sponging and ironing the beastly thing. It looks terrible. Lee puts it on with many grumbles, which become much worse when he discovers that his trousers will not do up round the waist. All my fault again, why do I give him so much starchy food, he's always telling me that we ought to eat more protein . . . protest at this that I *would* give him more protein if he would give me more housekeeping money, but this does not conduce to better relations and he crossly routs out old cummerbund, relic of his Air Force life in the Tropics. Final state of marital discord reached when it comes to his evening-shoes, which I had forgotten to tell him were seriously chewed by visiting puppy last summer. Hate puppy, hate all evening-clothes, hate Lee, and am fully prepared to hate this dance.

Say goodnight to children and Greta, now all harmoniously reading *Winnie The Pooh* in boys' bedroom. Would give a lot to change places with them. Do my best to assume expression of radiant anticipation to go with evening-dress and ask if they think I look all right? Greta enthusiastic, boys more reserved, James goes so far as to say I look like someone in a film (do not dare to ask *what* film, as he has only ever seen Westerns and Silly Symphonies), but Toby asks disapprovingly Whether I'm going to wear a Sweater? Say goodnight and kiss them all (except, naturally, Greta), and they say I Smell Peculiar. So much for expensive scent.

Downstairs find Lee in slightly better temper due no doubt to large glass of sherry which he finishes off guiltily when I appear, though unable to bend due to cummerbund. He says Well, if I'm quite ready? I am, and we go out to car. Lee shows tendency to stand about on doorstep saying What a Lovely Evening, have no patience with this and hurry on to garage, and am suddenly startled by tremendous crash from behind me. Turn round in astonishment to see Lee flat on his face on the gravel, having tripped over doormat. Laugh as heartily over this as I have laughed at anything for months. Dance, after all these preliminaries, quite an anticlimax.

*Tuesday, 23rd*

Late nights do not suit me. Try to think I look interestingly haggard but have to admit that Unkempt Blowsiness is fitter description. Great consolation however to be able to leave breakfast and children entirely to Greta, and concentrate on Lee, who goes off to work late and cross, and on clearing up bedroom which looks as though troupe of performing seals had been let loose in it. Get it more or less straight and have just put Lee's evening-shirt back in polythene bag preparatory to sending it to Chinese laundry when front door bell rings. Thrust polythene bag away in bottom of wardrobe and hurry downstairs.

Perfectly strange woman greets me effusively on doorstep saying that my friend Mrs Evershed has sent her. Suppose she is acquaintance of Susan's, cannot imagine why she has sent her to me or what I am to do with her at this unearthly hour, but summon what amiability I can and invite her in. Can hear Greta Hoovering in sitting-room and singing something operatic, so take stranger apologetically into kitchen. Breakfast things all over the place, fling them into sink and offer cup of coffee. Stranger accepts, and we drink tepid coffee and conduct rather stilted conversation. Cannot concentrate at all for looking at her; deep suntan make-up, inches thick, green eyeshadow, unnaturally auburn hair and very Voguish tweed suit with skirt so tight that I am quite surprised when she manages to sit down. Ben comes in, appears equally fascinated, and shows tendency to cling to Voguish tweed. Stranger says What a dear little boy and cringes away from him. Try to discourage him while continuing meaningless conversation. Hours and hours go by until stranger suddenly comes out into the open and tells me that she is a Glamour Expert. A *what?* A Glamour Expert, she repeats, Mrs Evershed thought I should be interested. (Wish Susan would leave my well-being alone.) Try to explain politely that such glamour as I have will have to get along without *expertise* from her or anyone else, but stranger sweeps my protests aside and launches out into obviously well-prepared speech about remarkable cosmetics she is prepared to sell me at fabulous cost, specially blended to meet my particular requirements, much patronised by American ladies (which she appears to regard as clinching argument).

Refuse everything, and say that I hardly ever use make-up. G. E. looks pitying and says she realises that, but that she has a very good Hormone Cream which many clients find helpful after a certain age; scientifically prepared, she adds earnestly, and used of course according to the directions as too much can have unfortunate effects. Assure her that we needn't worry on that score as I do not propose to use *any*, and get up in what I hope is dismissing sort of way. G. E. gets up too, but far from taking her leave says that she will just nip out to her car and fetch some samples, they are so attractively boxed. Could not care less. She adds with much fluttering of green eyelashes that she didn't bring box of samples in at first as I might have thought she just wanted to sell me something. Am too taken aback by this assertion to do anything but watch feebly as she trips out to nasty little pram-like car and fetches small suitcase, ardently followed by Ben.

Further hours elapse while she shows me contents of case, pots, jars and unguents of every description, all costing hundreds of pounds. Refuse everything but can feel defences getting weaker and weaker. Finally agree to purchase very small bottle of shampoo, hoping that this will get rid of her, but this very poor psychology on my part as she instantly takes fresh heart and starts offering me things for Lee. Hair tonic? Shaving cream? After-shave lotion? Spurn them all and say that My Husband uses an Electric Razor anyway. G. E. pounces on this and says Ah then she has Just the Thing, a lotion to apply before using an electric shaver which makes the bristles *stand out*. Never heard anything so revolting. Get rid of her at last by giving her Maybelle's address; an American, I explain, so she will be sure to be interested.

Nasty little pram-like car finally departs, to my great relief and Ben's evident disappointment. Hope his taste in women will improve in later years. Take back all I thought about Susan, can now absolutely understand circumstances which led her to send G. E. on to me, can only hope Maybelle will also be able to get rid of her.

Ring Susan later and tell her what I think of G. E. She agrees wholeheartedly and is even faintly apologetic which I consider encouragingly human. Take advantage of this to ask what about this baby? What news? Is it definite? Susan reverts to withdrawn voice, clearly pained by my vulgarity, and says that Really I do work things up so, do I never think of anything but babies, there are other things in life. Suppose I must infer from all this that she is not pregnant, great pity, a baby might take her mind off reforming me. Say Well I must ring off, Susan says so must she, and goes on to ask me if I would like to attend a series of lectures with her on Modem English Literature. Honest answer would be categorical No I would Not, but am as usual too much of a moral coward to say this, and stall by asking for further information. Susan instantly takes this as consent and says Next Friday evening, seven o'clock, she will call for me and Lee won't mind as he can talk to Greta. Ring off before she can tell me what we are to have for lunch, and plan headache for Friday night.

Rest of day passes in horrid haze. Greta has afternoon off and goes to meet aristocrat at Lady E-A's, children are ear-splittingly talkative at tea and tell me all about plans for

School Christmas Concert. Gather very confused impressions of this, according to James and Toby it is to consist of a Nativity Play in which James is to Take it in Turns being Joseph, while Toby recites *Calico Pie*. *Calico Pie*? I repeat, in a *Nativity* Play? But this, like every question I ever ask my family, goes unanswered while Toby goes on to tell me that Miss Young has said that perhaps he can be the Third Shepherd if he doesn't fidget. Mental picture of a fidgeting Third Shepherd reciting *Calico Pie* is too much for me and I leave them to finish their tea and remove Ben to his bath. Water stone-cold, remember too late that have not looked at boiler all day. On investigation discover that it is Out. Lee will be furious.

He is.


*Wednesday, 24th*
Feel normal again. Letter from B.B.C. confirming Voice Test for next week reminds me of forthcoming fame and glory and morale rises sharply. Plumber arrives to investigate possibility of installing Immersion Heater in hot-water tank. He becomes enthralled in system of pipes in house and follows them excitedly all over the place while Ben and I trail behind him. Plumber taps things with hammer and pokes about in obscure corners (shamingly dusty) and gets more and more enthusiastic. Am reminded of puzzles in book of Toby's, Find Your Way through the Maze Without Crossing a Line. . . . Plumber says When were these installed? and Cor he's never seen anything like it. Victorian he shouldn't wonder. Cor. Allow him what I consider sufficient time for admiration of all these wonders and when

I feel he must have had time to follow every antique tangled pipe to its conclusion refer him back to original question of Immersion Heater. Plumber laughs heartily and says Oh I won't want *that*, with this system it'd cost about Fifty pounds. Regretfully relinquish Immersion Heater. Plumber then says that He tells me what, that cold water tank isn't safe. Rotted underneath he's positive. Definitely. Saw one like it only last week, people tried to save cash, wouldn't take his advice, and what happened? What *did* happen? I ask agog. Well, stands to reason, says plumber triumphantly. Rotted underneath, just like he said. Definitely. The lady went out shopping, the tank collapsed, the whole house was flooded in no time. Plumber laughs heartily at this merry reminiscence and I remove Ben from below presumably lethal tank. Ask nervously if plumber thinks we ought to have a new one. He says that he Doesn't want to alarm me, but he does think I ought to switch off water-supply whenever I leave the house. Definitely. Cannot feel that I really want to be flooded out even when I am *in* the house, and ask nervously how much a new tank would cost? Plumber says Oh well, as to that he couldn't say exactly, but if my hubby would like a new one he could easily supply one. We agree to leave it at that, and hurry away from dangerous region. On point of departure plumber repeats that I *will* ask my hubby, won't I, as he wouldn't like to think of the damage all that water would do, not that he wants to frighten me. He *has* frightened me (though cannot prevent foolish notion that all that water might do a bit of highly necessary cleaning), and I assure him that Yes I will certainly ask The Doctor what he thinks. Am well paid out for this touch of pomposity as plumber's face lights up at mention of magic word Doctor and he comes back into the house, puts his bag down and tells me all about his recent sojourn in local hospital. Very remarkable and unusual operation was performed on him, nature of which he describes to me in unrestrained detail. Am only thankful that James and Toby cannot hear him, and pray that Greta is out of earshot, as nature of operation is very intimate indeed. Goes on for hours and hours and I run out of sympathetic comments long before he has finished, but this is immaterial as he is engrossed in his own recital. Stop listening and think about B.B.C. until he finally takes his leave.

Charming *divorcée* Ruth rings up in afternoon to say Can we come to Dinner on Saturday as she has some delightful University friends coming to stay who are dying to meet us. Know well that this is purest flattery, no reason on earth why delightful University people should wish to meet us, or if they do think so highly of us perhaps it would be better if we never met so that they can preserve their illusions intact . . . but suppress this ungrateful reaction and accept with enthusiasm. Tell Ruth about B.B.C. and she is unselfishly delighted and offers to accompany me on expedition to Voice Test.

*Thursday, 25th*
Suggest privately that Lee should take Greta to cinema this evening. Lee jibs heavily and says Why him? and adds, quite obviously on spur of moment, that he had been planning to Sort Out his work-bench. Disregard this as pure

moonshine, work-bench always has been chaotic and always will be, point out instead with what I consider to be great feminine guile that Greta will appreciate being escorted to cinema by good-looking man and that he will be able to translate complicated bits into German for her. Flattery as usual wins the day (am perpetually astonished that even intelligent men like L fall for that one every time), and I promise with great air of self-sacrifice to put children to bed so that they can get to cinema in time. True reason for wanting to get rid of both of them is that I have thought of splendid idea for Chapter Two of Book which I propose to spend nice peaceful evening writing.

This plan very nearly frustrated by children, who demand usual series of drinks of water, searches for Burglars Under Bed and final expeditions to lavatory, but get them installed eventually. Just as I am going downstairs James recalls me to ask What I would do if I was going for a Walk in a Wood and met a Wolf? Refer him to Little Red

Riding-Hood, but he brushes this aside as childish non-sense and tells me of plan he has evolved, should he ever find himself in this situation. He would, he tells me with great emphasis, have his rifle with him (provident child), and on sight of the Wolf he would run away *very fast*, but *as* he ran would fire rifle over his shoulder, and with *any luck* this should shoot the wolf, but even if it didn't he would be miles away anyway. This mixture of ingenuity and *sauve-qui-peut* rather impresses me, but refuse to prolong discussion and take my leave again. Toby bounces up indignantly in order to tell me what *he* would do to hypothetical wolf, but can guess for myself, he would bite it; beg them to Stop Talking Now, say Goodnight and leave them having animated conversation.

Sit down to write Chapter Two.

Write instead to Great-Aunt Elizabeth.

Draw a rather good horse on old envelope, but have trouble as usual with its hocks, and am eventually reduced to old device of making it stand in very long grass.

Tidy pigeon-holes of writing-desk and come across some fascinating old photographs. Admire these for some time, put them all together in separate pigeon-hole and feel business-like. (One advantage of being thoroughly untidy person is that it takes so little to give delightful glow of Feeling Efficient.)

Blank sheet of paper in typewriter reminds me of literary work. Ideas become fugitive, cannot imagine why I ever thought original notion so good, and relapse into unprofitable daydream in which I am giving a Book Talk at Harrods. Become concerned as to what I shall wear, and

finally abandon subject in favour of frightful mental melodrama which begins with car, Lee and Greta upside-down
in a ditch, and goes on through heartrending deathbed
scene to anguish of widowhood and anxieties about fend-
ing for my Poor Fatherless Children. At this point am in
floods of tears and not at all prepared to cope with return of
Lee and Greta, not in a ditch at all but very much alive. Lee
is concerned and says What on Earth is the Matter? at
which am horrified to note my own reaction is extreme
indignation with him for interrupting self-imposed orgy of
grief. Hope I shall never find myself in the hands of a
psychoanalyst. Mop myself up, apologise, and trust that
Greta has noticed nothing.

Later, over cup of tea, Greta is eloquent about excellence
of film, assures me that She has Understood All, and it is so
funny it has Make her to Cry. Lee says very little about
expedition except that Car is not going well, but am nervously aware that he seems more put-about than is justifiable
by this not uncommon state of affairs. All is explained after
Greta has retired to bed, when he bursts into impassioned
speech about how I am Never to make him do such a
thing again. But wasn't film good? I ask, knowing well that
this is not point at issue. Lee says Oh the *film* was all right,
what he could see of it. It was That Girl. He appears lost
for words and I am appalled and ask what on earth she did?
She behaved, says Lee bitterly, in way that he can only
describe as *un-British*. (Lee usually so tolerant, I am supposed to be the insular one, am astonished.) What did she
*do*? I ask again. Oh, she shrieked, she waved her arms, she
laughed too loudly, she exclaimed in German, he positively

had to disown her. Am torn between hearty laughter at picture conjured up, and sympathy for both of them. Mostly for Greta. Say as much, but Lee assures me grumpily that *she* enjoyed herself all right, and reiterates that I am never never to expect him to do such a thing again, it was in the three-and-nines too. Suggest bed before it can occur to him to deduct this from housekeeping money.

*Friday, 26th*
Parkinson's Law proved to the hilt in household affairs. (If P's Law is what I think it is.) Presence of Greta, far from lessening domestic chores, appears to have doubled them, and house looks no less squalid. Wish, as always, that I could achieve really intellectual approach to housewifery and disregard it entirely, but am as usual in uncomfortable state of feeling ashamed of prevailing slum-like conditions whilst being insufficiently competent or houseproud to do much about them. Am bound to admit that Greta, despite boundless enthusiasm and assurances of willingness, is slightly more useless than I am myself.

Intellectual exercise provided in evening by Susan and her lecture on Modern English Literature. Feel dreadfully guilty leaving Lee alone with Greta again, but he is unperturbed and says he really *is* going to sort out his workbench.

Lecture takes place in ice-cold hall, we sit in rows on uncomfortable benches and listen to young man with lock of hair expounding work of W. B. Yeats. Susan takes notes and looks intelligent. I take none and try to draw young man, but lock of hair surprisingly difficult. Young man draws extraordinary patterns on blackboard in order to explain Yeats' philosophy, and says much about Symbolism. Can understand nothing at all of any of it, and feel that Yeats is not for me nor me for Yeats. Young man becomes very worked up about some vital part of W. B. Y.'s scheme of things called a Gyre. Draws very odd squiggle to represent this and writes its name several times to be sure that we can understand. Dead failure as far as I am concerned. Can only think of *Jabberwocky* and 'gyre and gimble in the wabe' and mutter as much to Susan. She cannot hear, and we spend quite a long time hissing "*What*?" and "*Jabberwocky*" at each other. Very difficult thing to whisper, wish I had never embarked on it, particularly as it gradually becomes borne in upon me that (*a*) Susan has never read Lewis Carroll, and (*b*) lecturer has become aware of our inattention and has stopped talking in order to regard us with surprise. Are we in difficulties, he asks? Is this all too high-powered for you ladies? Furious at his patronising tone, would sooner die than admit I can't understand a word, and say No no, please go on, I'm so sorry.

Everyone else murmurs in similar vein, and lecturer does go on. Give up listening entirely, and look instead at rest of audience. Perfectly normal-looking women, cannot believe that they are *all* much cleverer than me, yet they all look as though they can understand it. Brain must have rotted more thoroughly than I had supposed.

Return attention to lecturer who has now finished with W. B. Yeats and is demolishing all contemporary writers. Dislike him more and more, particularly when he asserts that No good novels have been written in this country since the war. Nonsense. Cannot actually think of any with which to refute him at the moment, but feel sure I could some time when I am feeling less ignorant. Decide anyway to dash home and finish own masterpiece just to spite him. Do not mention this resolve to Susan on homeward drive, but cannot resist telling her that I did not think much of lecturer. She takes virtuous line that it was very interesting to *her*, as *she* doesn't know anything about Modern Poets. Implication that I think myself too well-informed on subject to need further instruction is aggravating. Assure her hastily that I don't know anything either, but that lecture has in no way altered this regrettable state of affairs. (Am however only too well aware that this fact will not prevent me from Knowing All About Yeats when I find myself back in company of Lee and Greta.)

*Saturday, 27th*
Life appears to be one long round of hectic gaiety. Lee complains bitterly and says Are we never to have an evening at home again? Consider this exaggerated, and can moreover foretell exact words with which he will complain next week, when no social events whatever are planned, that It really is getting Too Dreary for Words, the way we never go out.

Am much more concerned on Greta's behalf, feel that we should be staying at home to keep her company, but she assures me that she will be So Happy, she has work to do for Her Ladyship. Shows me English textbook of incredible complexity, can only hope she will not ask for help over it.

Dress to go out to dinner with Ruth. Feel that I must do her credit in eyes of charming University Professor, gaze at contents of wardrobe in vain hope that some garment will emerge looking rather less dowdy than hitherto. No choice really, select as usual black dress originally bought for long-ago honeymoon. (Cannot imagine why it still fits me, have always maintained to Lee that my Figure has been Ruined by Constant Childbearing.) Discover belatedly that hem of dress is unstitched and hanging down at the back, and make frenzied last-minute efforts to rectify this.

The bride wore black with touches of Sellotape.

Frustrate Lee in evident intention of wearing pink Leander tie, which may be distinguished but looks odd for dinner-party, cope with his inevitable reaction (If it's going to be a Dressy Affair he's not coming), persuade him into tie of slightly less distinguished but more colour-conscious club, and we set out.

Ruth lives in charming olde-worlde cottage in neighbouring village, with roses round the door, gay blue paint, wrought-iron lanterns and low beams everywhere. All very decorative and eminently suitable for the *petite* Ruth. Lee

and I both hit our heads with some violence on olde-worlde beams, and Ruth performs introductions. Charming University Professor and wife are both tall, grey-haired, and clever-looking, with stoops. (Wonder if stoops are there by nature or caused by contact with picturesque low beams? Or, perhaps more likely, brought on by lifetime's application to learned tomes. Phrase "scholarly bent" comes into my mind and am much struck by my own wit.)

Remember that Ruth has said that Professor and wife have been Dying to Meet us, feel that I must produce really original conversation so that they won't be disappointed. Rack brains unavailingly, can think of nothing suitable for Professor except that I was once at a University myself, which he will hardly find enthralling even if he believes it, which he probably won't as I find it improbable myself nowadays. Professor's wife however shatters illusion that in meeting me she is fulfilling a major ambition by confessing very nicely, while Ruth is out of the room, that she is So Stupid about names, would I mind just telling her all about who we are and where we come from? Toy with saying that we are here *incognito* and that The Press would never forgive me if I revealed our real names, but do not do so, and conversation proceeds along very familiar lines. Yes, my husband is a doctor, no he's not in practice, yes we have children, three little boys, yes they keep us busy, no I don't have domestic help, oh yes I do (had ungratefully forgotten all about Greta). Feel sure that Mrs Professor is as bored as I am by this conversation but we seem mysteriously unable to break away from it, indeed can see that she, like me, is listening with one ear to Lee and Professor who are being animated about, I think, Forensic Medicine. Perhaps I am safer on children and domesticity, but am impeded even on this subject by customary promise to Lee that I will not tell any funny stories about the children.

At this stage Ruth summons us to dinner, and I sit next to Professor and wonder what on earth I am going to say to him. *Not* Forensic Medicine at any price, but perhaps I could drag in about the B.B.C. and how famous I am shortly going to be? Before I can think up any way of saying this modestly, truthfully and entertainingly, Professor asks me very earnestly what my views are on Washing-up? Very nearly go home at once, but fortunately do not do so as he proceeds to give enthrallingly entertaining account of his own activities at the sink. Mrs Professor has, it appears, mental or physical condition which makes it imperative that she should sit down quietly for at least half an hour immediately after every meal. Look at her with respectful admiration. Professor, therefore, has taken over dishwashing entirely and has given much thought to the matter. (Hope Lee is listening.) He enlarges on his system and tells me passionately that married life would be quite insupportable to him were it not for a double sink, any amount of hot water and a plate-rack. Agree wholeheartedly (without revealing infinitesimal size of my own inferior single sink), and tell him about splendid little plastic cutlery-drainer recently acquired by me at Woolworths. Professor is agog, I obviously rise in his estimation, and he extracts notebook from his pocket and writes down details of cutlery-drainer all among presumably high-powered Professorial engagements. We eat superb dinner cooked by Ruth (cannot imagine why her ex-husband didn't know where he was well off), and conversation becomes general. Am emboldened to relate recent failure to understand philosophy of poet Yeats, and Professor is sympathetic and says he has always found it extraordinarily difficult himself. (Must tell Susan this.)

Remainder of evening passes all too quickly, and Lee and I congratulate one another warmly on our own conversational brilliance all the way home.

*Sunday, 28th*
Have uneasy conviction at belated breakfast that Milk Bill is thoroughly overdue, and that I have mislaid book of Tokens entitling Ben to Cheap Milk. Agitated search reveals that it is nowhere to be found, least of all in place where I have theory that I habitually keep it. Drive everyone distracted asking if they have seen it. Finally ask Greta if she has tidied it away somewhere, at which she stops burrowing in saucepan cupboard and confesses that she is not entirely certain what she is supposed to be looking for. Describe Token-book in graphic detail, and even go so far as to make little drawing of it on piece of grease-proof paper. Light dawns and she cries Ach yes this, she has Throw it Down the Well. Appears to think this is reasonable and helpful thing to have done. Am stupefied, and ask why she did that? She has think, she explains, that it is Old Cheque Book. Cannot begin to understand why she should think that this is desirable way to treat her employer's old cheque book, but she is now looking apprehensive, and dare not reprove her or she will burst into tears.

Ask Lee what is to be done. He says the Well is Thirty Foot Deep and any rubbish thrown down there has to stay there. James and Toby with one voice offer to descend into well to retrieve Token-book, and Lee says How often is he to tell them that they are not to go anywhere *near* well, and adds terrifying homily about Dangerous Gases to be found in it. James and Toby resentful at being deprived of splendid opportunity for killing themselves, and Ben drinks milk unconcernedly with little idea that it is probably the last he will ever have.

Sabbath calm shattered; if indeed it ever existed. Wonder what children will make of Dog Quoodle's "Smell of Sunday mornings" if they ever come across it.

Do not take James to church, as he wishes to go with his father in the evening (just an excuse for getting to bed late), and resist Toby's passionate plea to come instead. (Am I keeping his soul from his Maker? Possibly, but have had experience of Toby in church and am well aware that his vigorous activities there keep everyone else's souls utterly distracted.)

Visiting preacher takes the service and preaches impassioned sermon on Seventh Commandment. Glance round highly respectable village congregation and wonder what makes him think we are in any danger from fleshly lusts. Preacher obviously feels very strongly on subject and goes on far too long, shuddering histrionically and affectedly at bare idea of carnal sins. Whole performance rather irritating and, far from achieving desired effect, leads me off into rebellious view that I only wish opportunities ever occurred for me to have any chance of being tempted in this direction. Have practically decided to become Scarlet Woman, when I catch organist's eye by mistake and am recalled to myself. Wonder uneasily how much of recent flight of fancy was clearly visible on my face. Try hard to concentrate again on sermon, but preacher now well away on modern moral laxity about which he has nothing new to say, and I relapse instead into far-fetched daydream about Premium Bonds. Daresay preacher would disapprove of this too.

*Monday, 29th*
Wake up filled with splendid resolution to turn over new leaf and not be cross at breakfast-time. Now we have Greta there is no excuse, I am not overworked and I shall be calm, cheerful mother presiding graciously over breakfast-table, fully dressed and unhurried. Just as I am about to put this scheme into operation Greta knocks at bedroom door and says May she speak with me please? Find her on landing looking pallid and distraught, obviously unwell, but unable to explain to me what is wrong. Call on Lee to exercise his medical knowledge and his German; he remains modestly concealed behind bedroom door while I scurry from one to the other acting as very inefficient interpreter. Final diagnosis is that G is suffering from dear old friend Bilious Attack, known familiarly to Lee as D and V, and is to go back to bed until she feels better and on no account to do any cooking.

Good resolutions begin to crumble.

Beg children to hurry up, beg Lee to dress Ben, beg Greta to go to bed and keep warm, and hurry downstairs (far from fully dressed) to cook breakfast. Am just putting eggs on to boil (quickest thing) when James comes in and says Oh Mummy *not* boiled, he can't bear them. Hang on hard to calm cheerfulness and say Very Well darling, take saucepan off and substitute frying-pan (poached eggs). Toby comes in and says Oh Mummy *not* poached, he can't bear them. Swallow hard, determine to stay cheerful at all costs, and say in tones of suppressed fury, Very Well darling, have your cereal and I'll scramble them. Am just doing so when Lee arrives with Ben and says Scrambled eggs *again*? Give him look which I hope is eloquent and deal with Ben and bib in high chair. Ben gives one look at cereal and says No no no, and flings the lot on the floor. Everybody except me laughs heartily.

Good resolutions great waste of time, efficiency is the thing, a Bad Mother is better than No Mother. Continue to supervise meal without any further attempt at amiability.

Before leaving, Lee says What did I ever do about that woman who was so helpful when Ben cut his hand? Realise with horror that I have done absolutely nothing, not even found out her name. Decide to enlist help of the omniscient Mrs Parnell.

Greta remains in bed for morning but accepts cup of tea and dry biscuit and appears to be recovering.

Take Ben next door to seek advice on anonymous Good Samaritan from Mrs P who scrutinises scar on his hand with deep concern and tells me that Very Often these scars don't grow with the child and Deformity sets in. Pity, she adds, spoil things for him if he wants to be a Concert Pianist. Say that I don't think he *will* want to be a Concert Pianist, and Mrs P is rather shocked at my refusal to take the possibility seriously and says reprovingly that You never can tell. Interrupt her gloomy headshakings by saying briskly that what I *really* want is her help in identifying Good Samaritan, and recount entire story to her, as well as I can through her constant interruptions and those of Ben who is making repeated efforts to pick the paint off the front door. Finally hoist him on to my hip and ask if Mrs P can think who it could have been? Mrs P cogitates deeply and says Not tall you say? Wouldn't have been Mrs Roberts then? No, not tall. Short, like I said, with brownish hair and blue eyes and she said she lived up *that* way. Up that way? repeats Mrs P. Then it couldn't have been Mrs Pratt? No, it couldn't, Mrs Pratt perfectly well known to me and to everyone else in the village, she is the postmistress. Mrs P thinks some more and suggests several other people whom it could not have been, and Ben fidgets about and kicks me and begins to grizzle. Mrs P eyes him disapprovingly and tells me about her niece who had a great big boy like that, and *she* would keep carrying him about when he was big enough to stand on his own feet, very wrong it was, spoiling him, Mrs P often told her niece. Start to justify myself but get no further than Well, when Mrs P adds gloatingly And What came of it? Niece's spine was seriously damaged by carrying great heavy child about and she had to have it Transfused. (Extraordinarily unlikely operation, must ask Lee if there is any such.) Own spine gives ominous creak at this stage, put Ben down and turn to go home. Mrs P says in valediction that she's just thought who it might have been, and that she will make some enquiries and let me know. Reflect ungratefully that *I bet she will*, and go home to chores.

During shopping expedition in afternoon decide to buy box of chocolates to give Good Samaritan if ever I succeed in finding her, and go into newsagents to effect purchase. Am completely thrown off balance by finding that woman serving behind counter is in fact Good Samaritan in person. Cannot think of anything else to buy on spur of moment and can only select box of chocolates, receive them from her, pay for them and hand them back over the counter to her. Gracious and grateful speech which should have accompanied presentation is ruined, find myself blushing and giggling like idiotic schoolgirl, but Good Samaritan is delighted and grateful and carries whole transaction off very much more creditably than I do, and we part with many expressions of mutual goodwill.

Greta gets up rather tremulously for tea, and fortunately does not fully take in Toby's delicately expressed enquiry as to Whether she has Finished Sicking?

*Tuesday, 30th*
Remember that further rehearsal of melodrama is to take place in dining-room this evening, and send Greta out with Ben so that I can tidy things up a bit. Greta seems delighted at the prospect and says Ach that sweet Bennie, should she not try to make him speak now, yes? Assure her that she is welcome to try, my own efforts having been conspicuously unsuccessful, but after they have departed wonder nervously if she will teach him to say *Ach Gott nein*, which appears to be her favourite expression, or alternatively

whether I want him to learn to speak English with a strong German accent. Nothing however to be done about this now, so shelve the matter and devote myself to sorting out contents of extraordinary piece of furniture which I think is really a Victorian boot-cupboard and now serves (externally) as a sideboard and (internally) as a toy-cupboard. Owing to remarkable assortment of railway lines, bricks, cars, spades, stuffed animals, flying saucers, helicopters and Meccano this will now not shut, and there is nothing for it but to have complete and heartless clear-out. Decide to relegate once and for all every single thing that is broken to the dustbin. It very shortly becomes apparent that this is going to mean *everything*. Relent over the least awful, but nevertheless find myself carting armfuls of pitiful wrecks to their doom. Remainder still fills cupboard but at least door

will now close; feel virtuous and hope optimistically that children will not notice depredations.

Room, after subsequent cleaning operations, still looks terrible, though tidy. Decide that it is time we redecorated it, had rather got used to chocolate-brown paint on doors and skirting-board and hay-coloured walls and ceiling, but remember now that when we first occupied house we planned to brighten it all up. Decide that Lee can repaper it in his spare time. Children, when they return from school, *do* notice absence of beloved toys and are vociferous and indignant. Deceitfully pretend complete ignorance and spend much time and many subterfuges keeping them away from region of overflowing dustbin.

Lee says he *will* repaper dining-room on condition that I choose paper and buy everything and find little book on how to do it. Adds airily that he is Quite sure papering isn't very difficult, his aunts all do their own, and meanwhile will we all be quiet because he wants to Learn his Part. We are not all quiet a bit, but he remains huddled scowling over his copy of play, muttering to himself, while normal life clatters on.

Ask Greta what she would like to do while rehearsal is in progress, she is surprised and says But Her Ladyship has arrange, she is to go to *her* house. Suppose that this is really quite good idea as Greta and the Aristocrat appear to have become great friends, but wish that Lady E-A would not be quite so high-handed; do not say as much to Greta but suggest kindly that she Won't forget to take off her Apron before she goes will she? Greta is offended and says But this is her National Dress. Am apologetic, and she departs, apron and all. Lady E-A makes dignified arrival at this point, also in National Dress (well-cut tweeds and Pearls). Everybody else late, but finally all are assembled, only three-quarters of an hour after time appointed, and we begin.

Am delighted to get my own bit over early, and think I have performed creditably until Lady E-A says in dissatisfied tones Don't I think I could manage an accent? After all I am supposed to be a middle-European, let us just try that bit again.

We do it again and I attempt accent, and find myself talking, to my own ears at any rate, exactly like Greta. Everyone says Yes, Yes, that's just it. (How can I ever prevent Greta from seeing play?) Lady E-A says That was splendid, dear, we'll run through it again later if there's time (hope there won't be), but now she wants to work on that bit with Lee.

Retire to corner behind piano where Lady with odd skirt is already ensconced, as usual reading learned-looking volume. Try hard to see what it is but have much difficulty as she clutches it to her furtively when she sees what I am up to. (Can it be *Lolita?*) Eventually catch a glimpse of it and am surprised to see that it is in Latin. Am impressed by erudition of Odd Skirt.

Meanwhile Lee and Lady E-A are working out their destinies with much passion, am bound to admit that Lady E-A is excellent actress but think Lee looks very silly gazing at her so devotedly. Also he doesn't know his part. Lady E-A is indulgent about this and says Such a busy man, never mind, we'll go through it again, that'll help to fix it in his mind. They launch out into yet more passion, while remainder of cast fidget resignedly. Remove myself from vicinity of odd-skirted Latin scholar who is now mumbling feverishly over tome and eying me vindictively (I *think* she thinks I am reading over her shoulder, quite agree there are few more aggravating tricks but in this case it would avail me nothing anyway), and edge my way over to more attractive proximity of handsome man, name unknown. Unfortunately mistime edging manœuvres past Sarah Bernhardt and Henry Irving and receive tail-end of

passionate gesture by Lady E-A rather painfully in the small of the back. Everyone laughs except people most concerned, I am in considerable agony but nobody cares about *that*, and scene has to be begun all over again.

Spend remainder of it huddled up against window in frightful draught (Lee had better fix it when doing the room, that'll teach him to try to look like Yul Brynner), discussing redecorating project with handsome man.

Handsome man is pontifical, as well as he can be in hussing whispers, and asks if I want it Contemporary? Hiss back at him Er yes, er no, well sort of, but not very. *Gay*, really. Handsome man sneers slightly and asks scornfully What *is* this room anyway? Tell him that It is mainly the dining-room (cannot think when we last had a meal in it). He looks disbelieving, as well he may, what with nursery fender, child's desk, pair of stilts in the corner and calendar made by Toby hanging crookedly from large nail over the fireplace, but evidently decides to take me at my word and asks Well what is the Service? Am nonplussed by this. What *can* he mean? Does he want to know colour scheme of parlour-maid's uniform? Contemplate telling him we have fine old Renaissance-type butler, but light suddenly dawns and I realise he is referring to plates and things. Make rapid mental review of contents of kitchen china cupboard. Odd pieces of Cornish Ware, Pyrex, Willow pattern, Woolworth's enamel and Ben's Peter Rabbit mug hardly make up Service. Suddenly remember we still have a few plates left over from miscellaneous lot bequeathed to us by Lee's parents before they went to New Zealand, seldom used because cracked, and reply grandly that it is Mainly Spode. (Think it is Spode. One of those well-known names anyway, remember noticing it last time I washed them up, and being surprised.) Other members of the cast join in at this stage, and Fanny (looking sulky but charming in jeans) has much to say about Colour Values and Recessive Tones and contrasting wallpapers. She has just suggested dashing scheme in silver and black (quite idiotic, but pretend politely that I think it a splendid and practical idea), when we become aware that Lee and Lady E-A have finished their *pas-de-deux* and are looking emotionally exhausted and hopeful of applause. Give it belatedly. Lady E-A says in drained voice Now she wants us to be *quite honest,* have we any Criticisms? Only Fanny is brave enough to accept this at its face value, and offers various suggestions in highly technical language. Cannot myself ever distinguish left from right even in real life, let alone on the stage, and still less when stage is my own dining-room with all the furniture in the wrong places, but Lee appears to understand criticisms and accepts them courteously, while Lady E-A also understands them and disagrees with them all profoundly, with many venomous endearments. Situation threatens to develop, but is (as always) averted by Odd Skirt who tears herself away from *Hillard and Botting* and says She must be getting home to Mother. (Does she *have* a part in this play? Or does she just come to get a little quiet light reading away from Mother?)

Go to kitchen and put kettle on, and am just in time to catch sight of Toby whisking away to his room as I pass bottom of stairs. Pursue him and ask What he has been doing? He puts on great act of being half asleep, but on finding this does not deceive me becomes animated and says he Couldn't sleep and so has been sitting on stairs listening to play, and Daddy was Jolly Good. (Daddy's part as far as I remember consisted largely of confessions of a misspent youth, wonder how much Toby heard or understood. Not surprising he has nightmares if he often does this. Must try to make other arrangements about rehearsals.) Remake his bed, turn his pillow, and after much chat he finally subsides and I go back to offer tea to company. Find only Lee in dining-room, rearranging furniture.

Kettle boiling furiously in kitchen.

Sukey take it off again, they've all gone away.

*Wednesday, 31st*

Realise at breakfast that it is end of month and that new draw for Premium Bonds is therefore shortly due. Plan spending of £1,000 in some detail while spooning cereal into Ben, and only hear part of long technical speech by Lee about some new research project on which he is engaged. When he stops talking, presumably for congratulation and encouragement, am slightly dismayed to find myself replying dreamily that perhaps after all we Might Blue the Lot on a Mediterranean Cruise? Lee very nearly offended but fortunately is constrained by presence of children to repress what I think he would *like* to say, and only observes rather pityingly as he leaves the room that Really I just don't live in the same world as the rest of us. Perhaps I don't. How sad. Jerk myself out of reverie and bustle children off to school.

Later, when am in customary chaos of washing, consignment of coal arrives and I go to supervise it. Morning absolutely made by fact that coalman is handsomest man I have ever seen, blazing blue eyes and flashing white teeth in begrimed face hold me spellbound while his mate backs coal-lorry all over Lee's grass verges. (This will not be popular.) Coal is delivered, I lose count of sacks and coal dust flies in all directions; can only hope coalman is as honest as he is beautiful as have no idea whether bill is correct; accept it trustingly and notice at the same time that he is wearing rather nice black-and-white check shirt, exactly the kind I want for James and Toby for next summer. Ask him where he got it. Coalman appears flattered and launches into long speech, presumably telling me history of shirt, but unfortunately his Berkshire accent is very pronounced indeed and I am quite unable to understand a word he is saying. Try for one or two repeats but he is still no clearer and I cannot go on saying What did you say indefinitely, so have eventually to pretend that Now I understand, and thank him very much. Coalman, mate and lorry depart with final flashing smile and further inroads into grass verges, and I return to kitchen and washing machine. Greta is looking shocked by my familiarity with the Lower Orders, is the Aristocrat having a bad effect on her?

Washing takes much longer than usual owing to Lee's new Drip-Dry shirts, which he said would be such a boon to me. Have lost manufacturers' instructions but remember that there were a great many ways I *wasn't* to wash them, so do not dare put them in machine, but do them by hand in the sink instead with much toil and inconvenience. Am not allowed to put them through the wringer either, Drip-Dry being their very *raison d'être*, so seek out clothes hangers and hang them by the boiler to do their act. Large pool on floor by boiler very inconvenient, so transfer shirts to bathroom. (Trail of drips all up the stairs.) There is nowhere in bath-room to hang them. (Really my I.Q. must be very low, you'd think I'd know the equipment in my own bathroom by now.) Take shirts downstairs again and out to the clothes-line. High wind is blowing, splendid for everything

else but can see no way of ensuring that coat-hangers will stay on line in teeth of it. Bring them in again and ask Greta What she thinks? She doesn't think anything of any value. Lose patience with the tiresome things and put them through the wringer like everything else and hang them out with pegs in the normal way. (Shall just have to iron them while Lee isn't looking.)

Suddenly realise that appointment with B.B.C. is tomorrow and get agitated. Ring up Ruth and ask What on earth I should wear? Ruth is calming (all very well for her, she has broadcast several times), and advises me to wear Whatever I feel most at home in. At that rate, I assure her, I'll have to go up to London in old seaman's sweater and slacks. Splendid, says Ruth, why don't you? Beg her to be sensible, and ask if she thinks a Hat is desirable? Good Heavens, No, she shrieks, not unless I normally do, what do I think the B.B.C. is anyway, a Fashion House? Well no, I concede, but full of well-dressed and sophisticated people surely? No not a bit, says Ruth heartily, quite ordinary just like you and me. Do not believe this for one moment, and don't want to go if it *is* so. We finally agree that a coat-and-skirt is Always Safe, though Ruth is evidently disappointed by my lack of Bohemianism, and No Hat. Unless my hair is looking Too Frightful, I add at this stage, in which case I shall cover as much as I can with my only hat. Ruth appears to think I am deficient in clothes-sense, but beg her to leave me to it, I get quite enough education from Susan and I look how I look and that's all there is to it. Ruth says calmingly Yes yes, all right, she's sure I'll look very nice, and I realise that I have become shrill and cantankerous. Am rather gratified by this than otherwise, it must be my Artistic Temperament. Make final plans for trip to London tomorrow and ring off complacently.

Artistic temperament or no, nerves continue to descend on me at intervals for remainder of day and every time I re-read script I wonder why I ever thought it either funny, interesting or clever, and why the B.B.C. have been misguided enough to think so too. By tenth scrutiny it appears hardly to be written in English at all, and I contemplate sending telegram to B.B.C. cancelling appointment. Arrival of Lee dispels this idea as he says we Can't afford to send telegrams, will I instead look what he's brought home.

Produces a tape-recorder, borrowed from hospital.

Children are enthralled, and have to be told Not to Touch at least five hundred times, and we all make enthusiastic trial of it. Universal reaction is that it is very good of everyone else's voice. Am rather sorry for Greta, who is downcast about her German accent, but get very bored by humour of James and Toby who find it exquisitely amusing to say all their Worst Words into machine. (Worst Words, I am relieved to note, are not so very terrible; but still, joke wears a little thin long before they tire of it.)

We all spend much time trying to persuade the Trappist Ben to utter into it, he is full of willing smiles but as wordless as ever, until Toby pushes him impatiently away when he breaks into loud indignant protestations. These, on being played back, sound exactly like Donald Duck, and all are amused, including Lee, who evolves some merry scheme for leaving them on the tape so that they can be relayed to his Professor's secretary next day in lieu of Professor's official letters. (Sometimes think Lee's sense of humour is very little less primitive than that of his sons.)

After boys are in bed real object of tape-recorder is brought into effect and I read script for B.B.C. at it. Replaying fills me with gloom, voice sounds patronising, over-cultivated, middle-aged and monotonous.

Try the whole thing again, being bright.

Effect worse than ever, Arthur Marshall rallying school-girls, fruity and jolly.

Lee says soothingly It's all right really, try again, just saying it to *him*, forget about the B.B.C. and the recorder and all that.

Worst effect yet achieved, crooning cooing confidential note perfectly nauseating.

Evidently glamorous future as broadcaster does not lie ahead for me, had better make the most of this trip to Broadcasting House tomorrow as it is likely to be my last.

Lee says we had Better stop this, it is just making me self-conscious, and we cast care aside and discuss Great-Aunt Elizabeth's generosity, charm of Lady E-A (Lee has much more to say about this than I have), and plans for redecorating dining-room. Resolve to get this last done before next rehearsal in it, and enjoy pleasant vision of cast walking in and stopping in doorway with gasps of astonishment and admiration. Lee says Why don't I look at some wallpapers in London tomorrow? and I am indignant at suggestion that I should be expected to think about anything else but B.B.C. tomorrow. He says Well *after* the B.B.C.? Explain that after the B.B.C. I shall be either dancing with delight or in a furious rage of disappointment, and in neither case shall I be in a suitable condition to make sensible choice of wallpaper. Lee accepts this, and adds casually Did I realise that tape-recorder has been on all this time?

No I didn't.

We play it back and am at first impressed with wit and quality of our conversation until it gradually becomes apparent that on no single occasion have I allowed Lee to finish a sentence.

Am really rather sorry for him, married to me.

# NOVEMBER

*Thursday, 1st*

Meet Ruth on London train. She looks exactly right, faintly arty but not flashy, and I wish vainly that I were braver about colour of clothes. However, bright red probably more successful with Ruth's build than mine, had better stick to recessive schemes (like Fanny's wallpaper). Have defiantly put on only hat, and Ruth looks thoughtfully at it but makes no comment. She is evidently determined to keep me calm, is studiously non-provocative and spends journey (rather surprisingly) telling me all about Serious Operation she had when a small child and how she nearly Bled to Death. Am rather annoyed with her about this, who wants to hear about operations, and anyway the one I had after Ben was born was just as bad . . . tell her all about that as soon as I can get a word in edgeways, and long before it seems probable find that we have arrived in London. Ruth looks distinctly smug and I suddenly realise that she has successfully prevented me from thinking about forthcoming ordeal once until this moment. Very psychological these novelists are.

Customary cloud of provincial puzzlement descends upon me as soon as I set foot on London pavement, but Ruth will have none of my gaping rural nonsense and bundles both of us briskly on to a bus. She assures me that we have Plenty of time for a coffee before my appointment, but I feel this is rash, and say that I want to be there in *good time*. Ruth says competently that I shall be, it doesn't take an hour to get from here to Portland Place, we've time to do some shopping too if I like. Find this attitude positively irreverent, like buying sticks of rock at the gates of the Vatican, and refuse to shop. (Anyway I haven't got any money to spare.) We have coffee in small restaurant near Broadcasting House where Artistic Temperament (or something) reasserts itself and I have to retire to the Ladies *twice*, which Ruth thinks excessive.

After this I assert that Early or not early, we must go now. Knees by this time quite definitely knocking together, had always supposed this phenomenon to exist only in imagination of novelists, but this is quite real and indeed rather painful. Once in the street I become masterful and tell Ruth that we are now going to fulfil one of my Lifetime's Ambitions and before she can protest I hail a taxi, and demand The B.B.C. Please, in loudest and haughtiest tones I can manage. Driver conceals his surprise creditably (B.B.C. cannot be more than three minutes' walk), and we arrive at sacred edifice in style. (Very nearly as impressive a façade as that hairdresser's.) Ruth asks frivolously whether I oughtn't to remove my hat or my shoes or something before entering, and we arrive at reception desk giggling slightly, which I hope makes us look like Old Hands.

Charming receptionist greets us, asks name and business (Ruth retires modestly behind me at this point and breathes heavily and encouragingly down the back of my neck), I tell receptionist that I have an appointment with Miss Appleyard and that my name is what it is. She, well-trained woman, has courtesy neither to look blank nor ask me to spell it, and asks us to wait on sort of Out-patients bench while she telephones. Feel famous already, and Ruth and I retire and wait. I gaze about hoping to see Gilbert Harding while Ruth takes opportunity to give me last-minute advice. Powder your nose, fix that bit of hair, no, *that* bit, she hisses, twisting me frenziedly about. There, that's better, she thinks I look splendid, oh and I'm *not* to forget to *speak slowly*. Much, much slower than I even *think* is slowly. (All right, I know I gabble, will talk as to Greta.) And do remember, adds Ruth earnestly, that I am meant to sound as though I'm *talking* not *reading*. Promise to follow these instructions implicitly, that is if I'm not being violently sick by then which at the present moment feels probable, and continue to scrutinise stream of (presumably) Famous Voices coming and going through entrance hall, but none look in the least like Gilbert Harding or even Ruth Drew and am disappointed.

Waiting becomes agonising, if it lasts much longer shall have to visit the Ladies again, but when I say as much to Ruth she says firmly that That is Impossible (should be quite prepared to make substantial bet with her on this point), and adds, correctly, that delay is entirely my own fault for insisting on arriving quarter of an hour too early.

Eventually phone rings, and receptionist answers it and then summons me. Miss Appleyard will see me now, Studio WXYZ or something, do I know my way? (Subtle flattery.) No I don't. Receptionist says she will get a Page to guide me, and summons, apparently from the vasty deep, diminutive minion with acne. He clearly takes his role of Ariel seriously and whisks away with obvious intention of putting a girdle round the earth in far less than forty minutes, and I sprint breathlessly in pursuit, waving a hasty farewell to Ruth. Ariel leads me at breakneck pace into and out of lifts, along corridors, into street and back again, over hill over dale thorough bush thorough briar, and finally deposits me, breathless and voiceless, in padded cell. He then departs, back to the vasty deep, and I take stock of padded cell. General impression is of green paint, dangerous-looking machinery (Do Not Touch, 5,000,000 Volts . . . all right, I won't), and one wall all made of plate glass looking out on to blackness. (Am I under observation?) This notion causes me hastily to snatch pocket-mirror out of my handbag to see what I look like. Result not encouraging, I look distraught and Ruth was quite right, hat *was* a mistake. Do my best to rectify matters but with little hope of success, and cell door opens and in comes Miss Appleyard.

(Oh dear, she is small. I do wish there were more women of my own size about.)

She greets me breathlessly (can she also have been following Ariel?) and says she's terribly sorry to have kept me waiting, but she has been at the Tower of London. (How *extraordinary*.) She does not, however, explain this but gets briskly down to business. Come along into the Studio. (Thought I was in it.) Lights are turned on in all directions, and studio appears on the other side of the plate glass; we transfer ourselves, rather like Alice through the Looking Glass, technician appears and takes over amongst the dangerous machinery, and Miss A sits me down at large table. She eyes me beadily and says in tones of one accustomed to incompetence that She doesn't suppose I have a copy of my script? Well sucks to her, I have. (Do not, naturally, put my reply in quite those words to her.) She is pleased with me, and tells me to be Having a Quick Look at it and be removing the paper clips while she gets things ready. Get script out of handbag, drop it, pick it up, remove paper clip and drop *it*, scrumple pages up and smooth them out and get them in the wrong order and otherwise generally occupy myself in controlled and orderly fashion while Miss A indulges in curious tic-tac communication with technician beyond the plate glass.

At last all is said to be ready, and Miss A says Go ahead, just read it quite naturally as though you were talking, don't hurry. Confused memories of yesterday's session with tape-recorder and Ruth's advice lead me to start off in slow high tones rather like a Duchess opening a bazaar. Every now and then there is a bit which I hope is funny, when Duchess-like tones become unsuitable and I revert to normal gabble, but feel that this is wrong too, and quickly put in More Expression. Entire performance seems to take hours and hours and must sound like someone doing Impressions. Hardly dare look at Miss A when it is over. She says Yes, that was all right, but does not look as though she means it. Indeed she obviously *didn't* mean it as she goes on to point out, quite kindly, all the things I did wrong; main fault apparently was that I was far too slow, talk should have taken six minutes and in fact took nearer ten. (Suppress unworthy reaction that since B.B.C. pay one by the minute this is all to the good.)

Try it again, says Miss A, and go at your normal speed.

(*What* I think of Ruth and her advice.) Am just about to start when she adds, Oh, and don't drop your voice at the ends of sentences. Very well. We try it again and achieve better results. Technician nods and smiles encouragingly through plate glass and Miss A says That was Much Better. Shall I, then, will I, can I, I stutter excitedly, *does* she think I shall be required to broadcast it? At this indelicate enquiry Miss A goes all withdrawn and secretive and says Ah well, as to that, she *hopes* to get it taken, certainly They thought highly of it Up There. (Up where? Heaven?) It will all depend on Them, and she will let me know very soon.

Can only keep my fingers crossed and hope that They, whoever They are, will give favourable verdict and moreover that They will have good feeling to select a date in termtime if I am required to broadcast.

Miss A appears to have no more to say to me nor I to her, and she asks if I know my way back to the Entrance Hall? Not if it means route patronised by Ariel I don't; Miss A is therefore morally obliged to escort me back to Ruth, which she does to the accompaniment of very laborious conversation. How many children have I, how old are they, and where did I say I lived? Answer appropriately, and Miss A says dutifully, but without much conviction, What nice ages and That's a lovely part of the country, after which we both relapse into silence. Suppose it is difficult for these Career Girls to know what to say to Provincial Housewives, and certainly I am being no help, but am nevertheless depressed. Finally reach Entrance Hall and Miss A and I part with, I think, mutual relief.

Ruth is welcoming and encouraging and under her

sympathetic influence am very soon full of optimism again and we spend cheerful lunchtime at Lyons deciding what records we shall choose when invited to take part in radio programme *Desert Island Discs*, and am only slightly dashed when Ruth says Will I now kindly *stop* raising my voice so affectedly at the ends of my sentences as she is not Miss Appleyard.

*Friday, 2nd*

Do not appear to have won £1,000 on Premium Bond. Disappointment too familiar to be very profound. Cast dreams of wealth and fame temporarily from my head and revert to normal domesticity. Clean bedrooms with assistance of Greta and Ben, and am hard put to it to say which of them is least help, as Ben at least understands most of what I say to him and sometimes obeys, though wordlessly, whereas Greta understands little and is far from wordless. By Elevenses Time we are all exhausted, and I send them out for a walk. Weather very unattractive, poor Ben as usual has choice between summer coat which fits but is not warm, and cast-off duffle-coat of Toby's which is too big, and one of his gloves is missing. (When I am rich I shall buy all my children complete new wardrobe the *right size*. They will be unrecognisable.)

After they have gone settle down to session of cooking, as we have children coming in to tea and fireworks tomorrow. Bitter experience has taught me not to bother with traditional cakes and jellies as present-day children never seem to eat anything like that, and make instead quantities of biscuits, cheese-straws and sausage-rolls. Listen at the same time to *Mrs Dale's Diary* on wireless and am annoyed when telephone rings so that I miss some.

Telephone is Lady E-A. Will we all come to tea on Saturday week? First impulse is, regrettably, to say No we won't, but stifle this and say We should love it. That nice husband of mine too, says Lady E-A urgently, and don't dress up, the children can play in the garden. (In November? Is she mad?) Know very well that we shall all dress up like anything, Lady E-A lives in Stately Home with parklike grounds and has quantities of minions before whom our normal appearance would be out of the question. Nevertheless thank her again, assure her that we shall come Just as we Are, and am about to ring off when Lady E-A adds Can she ask me a Great Favour? (If it is to take

Lee on a Yachting Cruise, no she can't.) Will I be very kind and take pity on some Americans who have just arrived in the district and don't know anyone? Yes, of course I will. I will ask them to coffee one evening (cheaper than a meal). Lady E-A blesses me fervently and tells me all about antecedents of Americans, long elaborate story about a sister in Horton, Michigan, and sister's husband who is In Oil (like a sardine) and sister's husband's cousin who is Godmother to wife of these people who are over here on Cultural Exchange. (What on earth is Cultural Exchange?) Assure her anyway that I shall be delighted to foster Anglo-American relations to this extent, thank her again, and ring off. Resolve to ask Maybelle and Cliff to join party in order to make unknown Americans feel more at home.

Return to kitchen to find *Mrs Dale* finished, but wireless now playing music from *Giselle* which delights me, and presently causes me to spring about kitchen, potato-peeler in hand, with many an ambitious *jêté* and *tour en l'air*. Greta and Ben return unexpectedly and catch me at it and I feel foolish, but they join in with enthusiasm, we all caper madly, and the last batch of biscuits burns neglected in the oven.

On return from school James and Toby have again much to say about forthcoming school concert, James by his own account is uncertain whether, in the Nativity Play, he is to take part of Joseph, Mary, the Babe, or one of the Animals. Or he might be a Shepherd. He *could*, he says, do any of them, he is rather Good at Acting. Am reminded of Play Scene in *Midsummer Night's Dream*, and say he is a proper little Bottom, isn't he? To my horror both children take this

entirely in the wrong sense (hardly surprising really, they have never even heard of Shakespeare) and go off into transports of shocked but delighted laughter. Have probably acquired reputation of bawdry now with my children which will last a lifetime. Only hope they will never see fit to write autobiographies.

Lee arrives home late, having made purchases of dozens of fireworks for tomorrow's party, and has much to say about expense involved. Adds that he has decided next year to Make them himself, perfectly easy and Much Cheaper.

Am horrified and beg him to do no such thing, adding perhaps tactlessly that if he is so keen on Do-It-Yourself what
about redecorating the dining-room? Lee replies touchily
that there's no need to nag, he hasn't forgotten, he *said* he
would do it and he's *going* to do it, in fact he has actually
brought home some samples of wallpaper, come to think of
it, where on earth are they? We search about and finally run
them to earth under seat of car, with large muddy footprint
on back of one.

He, Greta, and I spend much time looking at samples,
taking it in turn to hold them up against the walls and
stepping back to get the effect. Greta favours bold stripes,
Lee prefers more cautious mottled affair, and I am unable to
decide between highly contemporary squiggles, and old-
fashioned roses-and-medallions. Lee says crushingly that
he thinks this last looks more suitable for a maid's bedroom and I wonder if Greta will think this is slighting
reference to her, and am at once compelled to comfort her
(probably nonexistent) wounded feelings by lending my
support to Bold Stripes. Lee says stripes will be very difficult to hang, better wait and see what they all look like by
daylight. Anyway, he adds with unprecedented energy, no
reason why he shouldn't make a start now Stripping the
Walls. Scream loudly at this suggestion, and say For
Heaven's Sake not till after the party tomorrow, and Greta
chimes in with usual Ach Gott nein! which irritates me as
much as ever, no less so when it occurs to me that it is
more or less what I have just said myself. Lee says Really I
am a bit hard to please, and retires to sitting-room with *The
Lancet*; Greta joins him with English textbook, how

studious they are, shall take opportunity to iron Drip-Dry shirts in furtive sort of way with kitchen door shut.

*Saturday, 3rd*
Collect wood from all over garden to make bonfire. Add contents of dustbin for good measure; very very short-sighted move as children pounce on *débris* with loud cries and rescue beloved toys. They express much innocent astonishment as to how such treasures could ever have got on to the bonfire, and carry armfuls of broken horrors lovingly back into the house. Am not sufficiently strong-minded either to own up or to insist that rescue operations should not take place. Good and peaceful result however has been inadvertently achieved, in that all three become engrossed. Toby retires to private world with headless soldiers and small cannon with no wheels, James immerses himself in torn Annual, and Ben sits contentedly on embryo bonfire with half a helicopter.

Ring Susan and ask her if she would like to come and watch fireworks. Very much a children's party, I warn her, but if she would *like* to come? Susan says Yes she would, very much, as it happens she has her two little nieces stay-ing with her, could they possibly come too? Yes of course they could (*think* dining-room table will take two more, only hope nieces are small). Susan then says that she must ring off, no time to gossip, her Daily Woman hasn't turned up today and really there is so much to do. Express civil, but not very heartfelt sympathy, and she goes on to tell me that there were the Beds to Make and the Laundry to Count and the House to be Cleaned *and* the Lunch to be

Got, really it is quite *impossible* and she's never been so exhausted in her life. Very likely she hasn't, but am hard put to it not to point out that this story of terrible toil is nothing to the daily lot of most of us, and to get her off the subject ask to be told more about the nieces. Penny and Elizabeth, says Susan, only always known as Penny and Farthing. (Very whimsical, can hardly wait to hear Lee's reaction to that one.) They are eight and six, she goes on, just the same ages as James and Toby, and she expects they'll all make Great Friends. (She can't ever have heard J or T on the subject of Girls if she really thinks that.) They are also, she assures me with no false modesty, very pretty, very intelligent and amusing, and unusually well-behaved. They sound odious. Nevertheless say that I shall be delighted to see them this afternoon, and add Well I mustn't keep you (really meaning that I want to get away myself), and am just about to ring off when Susan lowers voice to confidential murmur and says she has been wanting to ask me, Lee will know if I don't . . . heart sinks at this familiar opening, and rightly so, as Susan proceeds to ask me long complicated and intimate question which should more properly be addressed to her gynaecologist. Wish passionately, for the millionth time, that Susan wouldn't assume that marriage to a doctor automatically brought with it unlimited knowledge of medical matters. Am full of sympathy for her in her wish to have children, but really feel that she must go about it like everybody else, no good asking me for Short Cuts. Try to answer her repressively but kindly, but she goes on and on and on, and I stop listening and deal with Toby who is now scuffling round my feet with soldiers and cannon saying Bang-Bang. One of the bangs catches me rather sharply on the ankle and I am not pleased. Finally Susan interrupts herself by screaming Help the potatoes are Boiling Over, she must *fly* (had no idea it was so late, ours aren't even on yet, unless Greta has had the sense . . . no, she hasn't . . .), and am at last able to ring off.

Children's party goes well on the whole. James' and Toby's school friends arrive in large expensive cars, and show a tendency to have mothers in Fur Coats and Pearls, but these luckily hurry away and their offspring are perfectly normal and untidy, and heavily armed to a boy. Only girls present are Penny and Farthing, who arrive escorted by Susan, all looking too immaculate for words. P and F are pretty but shy, feel rather sorry for them among hordes of little boys who are now all busy shooting and shouting. (Can hear Lee monotonously repeating Don't point guns at people, point them at the ceiling . . . but with very little effect.)

Sit them all down to tea.

Slight diffidence over beginning to eat is quickly dispelled and enormous bowls of potato-crisps and hot sausages disappear like magic. Greta and Susan bustle about helpfully fetching more, cheese-straws are suspect at first

until Toby, with air of great bravery, samples one and gives favourable verdict (with his mouth full). Plate of cheese-straws is instantly emptied. Am gratified by popularity of food provided but cannot help feeling that Table-manners of children of today would shock Grandpapa badly. Still, am comforted to observe that my own children, though hold-ing their own, are not the worst; have indeed to speak quite severely to seven-year-old redhead who has evolved screamingly funny and original idea of throwing scones with honey on them at the ceiling. Fortunately redhead obeys me before practice becomes widespread, though James gives me dark look and obviously considers me a Terrible Spoil-sport. Offer redhead chocolate biscuit instead, and everybody says Gosh, chocolate biscuits, where? Where indeed? Cannot see them anywhere. Finally discover that Penny and Farthing, whom I have put either side of Ben in his high chair in hopes that they will look after him in Womanly Way, have between them *finished* the chocolate biscuits and the three of them look thoroughly bloated, chocolatey and guilty.

Lee, who has been coping with drinks, interrupts at this stage to say that If anyone wants any more to drink it will have to be orange or lemon as the Milk is Finished. Am appalled at this, they weren't supposed to drink milk *at all*, that was for cocoa after fireworks, children always want Squash at tea-parties, *not* milk. Lee, when I explain this to him in a furious stage whisper, says apologetically, Yes, he knows that, he was going to give them squash, but one little boy said he wanted milk, and then they *all* wanted it. (Bet it was that redhead, an individualist if ever I met one.)

Redhead at this stage looks up with angelic smile and says Pleathe can he have thome more thothigeth? Both front teeth are missing, which makes him almost incomprehensible but very engaging, forgive him and present him with another sausage. (Awful thought here that I don't believe his teeth were missing when he arrived. Hope his mother won't mind.)

In incredibly short space of time table is bare of food, though covered with as much litter as a fairground, and tablecloth will never be the same again (five spills), and I hustle children away to Wash their Hands and put on Warm Clothes. All are amazed at suggestion of washing, never heard of such a thing in their lives, but I am adamant, and insist on that and other bathroom rites. At length all are wrapped up as for Arctic Expedition and Lee heads for bonfire, bearing box of fireworks and accompanied by yelling escort, armed to the teeth.

Establish Greta and Ben at upstairs window to watch fireworks, Farthing elects to stay with them and Susan and I do what we can with mess in dining-room. Three guns and two sandals under the table, also half-eaten sausage-roll and a scone well ground into the carpet, frightful mess of chocolate on high-chair and quantity of unfinished mugs of milk keep us fully occupied. (Shall save milk; unhygienic, and Susan is shocked, but cannot help that.)

We decide to leave washing-up, as Lee by this time probably going mad. This supposition proves correct. Bonfire is going well, and all the little boys (and, presumably, Penny, who in trousers and duffle-coat is indistinguishable) are doing their best to cremate themselves in it. Loud screams are continuous, and from time to time two or more boys coalesce and become embroiled in fight apparently to the death. Hope none of the guns are actually loaded.

Lee greets our arrival with relief and says he will now Start Fireworks. Says this quite quietly, and amidst uproar I can hardly hear him, but little boys all hear distinctly and converge upon us with many offers of help. Lee refuses them all and shepherds them back to stand in comparative safety behind the cabbage-patch. (About as effective as King Canute stemming the tide.) Rockets, Roman-candles, and Golden Rain are set off with triumph and we all exclaim and admire delightedly. Catherine-wheel nailed on to apple-tree less successful, very sulky and spasmodic performance, and James is annoyed when I will not let him go and spin it round by hand. Horrible objects which zigzag frenziedly about on the ground, hissing and banging, are wildly popular, as are sparklers, which children are allowed to hold themselves. (They appear disappointed to find that they are unable actually to set fire to one another's clothes with these, but this does not deter them from keeping on trying.)

Catherine-wheel surprises us all, when we had quite forgotten about it, by going off with unprecedented vigour, and finally coming loose from its moorings and sailing dramatically over our heads. (Wonder what effect it will have on American Blight?)

Bonfire by now is dying down, and I become aware that I am very cold and that it is beginning to rain. Round up children to come indoors; this takes ages, as I cannot see my way in the dark and stumble painfully over various

miscellaneous objects, and waste a good deal of time calling Gooseberry Bush to Come along now, under impression that it is Small Boy.

Greta and Farthing are complimentary about firework display, Ben is said to have enjoyed it, and Greta has cleverly produced enough cocoa for children, which they consume in kitchen while I run Field-Dressing Station at sink dealing with series of minor abrasions. No child appears totally unscathed, but all injuries are result of natural hazards, not burns, so I feel that this is Just Life and not our fault.

Parents of visitors arrive in Jaguars and Landrovers and Lee entertains them with sherry in sitting-room. (Always feel this custom very unfair; *they* don't need drinks, *they've* had a lovely peaceful afternoon without their offspring;

interesting too to note cynically that it is always the fathers who come to fetch their children on these occasions.)

At what feels like midnight Susan and all the parents depart, children all say (with much heavy prompting) Good-bye and thank you for having me, and disappear into the night.

We agree that house and garden will probably never get back to normal but that it has all been a Great Success. Greta says This is an Interesting English Custom and asks if I will tell her All About Guy Fawkes. Not tonight, Josephine.

*Sunday, 4th*

Children, having gone to bed much later than usual last night, wake up unnaturally early as is their inconsistent habit. Am not at all pleased by affectionate morning greeting from James and Toby at half-past six, beg them to go back to bed and not to wake Ben. They depart offendedly, but recur at fifteen-minute intervals saying Surely it's getting-up time *now*? Loud thumpings from Ben's room indicate that he *has* been woken up. Try desperately to go on sleeping in hopes that Lee will cope, but he remains huddled determinedly under bedclothes and at fifteenth arrival of boys I take line of least resistance and tell them to go quietly down to kitchen and get biscuits for themselves and Ben. (Very bad for their teeth and their discipline but I *must get some sleep.*) Comparative peace reigns after this, at least noise remains *outside* bedroom door and is harmonious, but sleep meanly refuses to return. I am wide awake, ice-cold, and very cross, and may as well Get Up. Do so, feeling like a martyr, and decide to give Greta her breakfast in bed just to prove how ill-used I am. Bump several times into Lee's bed, not by mistake at all, until he has decency to wake up too. (He couldn't *possibly* have been really asleep all this time.) He says he May as well have a Bath, as we're so early, and goes to have it. I go down to kitchen, calling in on boys *en route* to suggest that they join Daddy in bath-room, they can Wash his Back for him. (This is purest malice on my part, am rather ashamed of myself.)

Prepare breakfast. Am surprised to discover that it is not at all early any more, clocks are totally unreliable but B.B.C. has already got going on *Home For The Day*, which means it is well after nine o'clock, what can have happened to all that time? Whilst stirring porridge am interested to hear talk by Well-known Woman Novelist, who asserts that All Creative Artists are Very Lazy, and find it a terrible effort to

Get Down to Work. Am much encouraged by this, and feel that I have at least one qualification for becoming Well-known Novelist myself.

Lee and boys take hours and hours to appear, despite repeated bellowings to Hurry Up by me, and am just about to dash upstairs and nag when Lee makes dramatic appearance looking pale, reels to a chair and sits down with his head bowed between his knees. Good Heavens, I shriek, Are you Ill? (Very silly question really, he is obviously on point of expiry.) He shakes his bowed head and presently sits up and leans back, still looking wan but slightly better, murmuring that it's Quite All Right, Better in a Minute. Weak voice and air of self-deprecation alarm me more than ever, look round frantically for something reviving to dash in his face, but only handy thing is boiling porridge which I think better not to apply. James and Toby arrive, and much heavy breathing and thumping on stairs indicates imminence of Ben. Wonder if I should hustle them all away from spectacle of their moribund father, but Lee becomes brisk again and says he is Better. But what was it all about, I ask, what happened to you? Lee says solemnly that he Very Nearly Fainted, and do I know why? No, I don't, why? Because, he assures me, he has just Made All the Beds. He had no idea this was such a frightful and exhausting task, and he is never going to do it again, and he doesn't think I'd better either. Can only promise insincerely that I never will (rather hard on Greta if I kept to it), and morale rises sharply at reflection that mine is evidently more hazardous calling than I had hitherto supposed. (Have a good mind to ask, at some more suitable moment, for Danger Money to be added to Housekeeping Allowance.)

Give Church a miss, but feel thoroughly guilty when bells ring and hatted procession of more conscientious Christians is to be seen going down the road clutching prayer-books. Mrs Parnell is last of these, sporting new expensive-looking fur coat. She looks at my old slacks in surprise and asks What I am doing? (Garden-fork in one hand and rake in the other should make it fairly obvious I should have thought.) Reply that I am trying to Tidy the Garden Up a bit, and Ben appears and makes Donald Duck noises. Mrs P looks at him disapprovingly and says Still not Talking? Backward isn't he? Maternal pride is incensed, and I tell her that On the Contrary, Ben is the most intelligent of my children in many ways. (Difficult to adduce much evidence for this, but am sufficiently illogical to be prepared to make same claim for any of the three of them on equally inadequate grounds.) Mrs Parnell looks disbelieving and asks if I enjoyed myself in London the other day? Never told her I was going, but am used to her omniscience, and tell her about the B.B.C. Oh, just something lit'ry was it, she says disappointedly, and hurries after tail-end of church-going procession. (Wonder if she thought I was going for Illicit Assignment, and if so why she should suppose I would tell her about it?)

Spend, unwillingly, remainder of daylight hours (mercifully few) gardening. Lee does Autumn Digging and says that he really rather enjoys it once he gets going, and seems to think I am rather unpatriotic not to become equally reconciled. Remain convinced that there is nothing whatsoever to be said for cold, dirty, uncomfortable and unrewarding occupation on which I am engaged. (Digging up flower-bed that never had any flowers in it, and never, as far as I am concerned, will.) Toby joins me and tells me that he has Discovered What it Is about Grownups. What *what* is? I ask stupidly. Well, he says earnestly, the thing is that grownups are Terribly Nice to you, they tell you that they love you and all that and sometimes even *kiss you* (tones not entirely appreciative of this privilege), and *then*, all of a sudden, they get furious and send you to your room and you mustn't come out till you've said you're sorry. For *No Reason*. Do not like to spoil this outburst of confidence by taking opportunity to explain cause and effect, but am nevertheless much enlightened and realise that my disciplinary efforts will have to be entirely remodelled.

Lee spends much of evening lighting boiler, addressing it in uncomplimentary terms and relighting it, and in telling me that if we don't do some entertaining soon we won't get asked to a Single Party this winter. (Does he really want to go to a single party? I don't. Perhaps if I were slim I should. *Must* diet.) Agree, however, that we must give a party ourselves, and this reminds me of unknown Americans to be entertained on behalf of Lady E-A. This in turn makes me think of Finance (coffee very expensive, wonder if they'd like to see how the English live and have Tea instead?), and finance reminds me of B.B.C. and I wonder if there will be an offer to do broadcast in the post tomorrow. Final link in train of thought is reached at this point when consideration of tomorrow reminds me that it is day that Plumber is due to instal new cold-water tank. Tell Lee that he needn't have bothered with boiler as we have to let it out tomorrow anyway. As he has just got it going after sixth attempt he is not pleased, and says several things about it (and me) that Greta overhears.

Take opportunity to tell her later that she mustn't use those words herself, and apologise on Lee's behalf, at which Greta clasps her hands and says she Understands so! and the Doctor he is Wonderful, isn't it?

(*Is* it? Am more often inclined, myself, to think it is very aggravating.)

*Monday, 5th*

Much time spent preparing for advent of Plumber; rather like getting ready for prolonged siege. Lee takes much trouble putting boiler out, for once needless to say it is going like a furnace in the morning instead of being in its usual last-gasp condition, and Greta and I hurry about filling every receptacle with water before Mains Tap is turned off. Bath, basins, buckets, jugs and sink all brought into use (can we possibly be going to need all this much?) and Lee says Now we shall be All Right, and proceeds to turn off Mains. (Tap situated in peculiarly inaccessible corner of store-room behind all the trunks.) He is just about to depart when unmistakeable sound from upstairs w.c. causes him to exclaim angrily That Girl's gone and Pulled the Plug, and Greta gets sharp reproof from him. She is not unnaturally highly embarrassed, and I hustle Lee away, assuring him that None of us will do it again. (Can foresee that this is aspect of affairs that is going to be very inconvenient indeed. Just as we were getting Ben so well-trained too. Wonder if Susan would like to have us for periodic visits during the day?)

Plumber duly arrives with Mate, who looks about fourteen, and is speechless (should get on well with Ben), and they climb about old tank while plumber says Cor, yes, just like he thought, it's in a shocking state. No cover on it neither, he doesn't like to think what's been getting into our drinking water. (Remember Greta's recent *malaise* with some guilt.) Old tank is finally emptied, disconnected and removed, and Plumber and Mate stagger downstairs with it with many groans. They place it outside the back door

and we all look solemnly at it. Looks perfectly solid to me, though agree that It is Dirty, but Plumber kicks it scornfully and seems to think we have had more than our fair share of luck in avoiding disaster from it. Rolls himself a cigarette, and takes his ease against the back door surveying garden patronisingly. Nice place we've got here. Definitely. Though he Tells me What, we ought to get some of those trees down. They'll be undermining the house. Goes on at great length to tell me all about acquaintance of his who had house very like this . . . trees in garden very like this . . . roots got under foundations and what happened? Cracks. Great cracks big as your arm in side of house. Cor. We all look nervously at side of house expecting to see cracks appear (actually there are several, but luckily they are on further side of house and shall keep plumber away from there if I die in the attempt), while Mate kicks tank shyly, evidently feeling it is required of him, but still does not utter. Plumber finishes cigarette, grinds it out on the path before I can stop him, and says Well well this isn't getting anything done. Looks again at old tank and says hopefully That'll do very well there, won't it, just nice for the Kiddies to Play in. Very sorry for him, I know it's horribly heavy, but am forced to admit that it won't Do Very Well there at all as no one will be able to get in or out of the house. It is accordingly moved to site of James' abortive swimming-pool, and plumber looks injured and clasps his back with both hands with agonised expression. Suddenly remember saga of his Operation, and say hastily that We'll leave him to it now, as we are going out for a walk.

Go down the road to call on Susan.

She is interested to hear about Plumber, gives us coffee
and tells us that we are welcome to come and Pull her
Plug all day if we want to. Eventually arrange to leave Ben
and Greta with her for remainder of morning while I go
back and supervise activities of Plumber and Do Something
about lunch.

No sign of Plumber when I return home. Van gone,
house silent. Very surprised, go upstairs to see if New Tank
is installed. New tank is installed all right, but experience
quite frightful shock at sight of apparently inert body of
Mate dangling from it, feet first, swinging but silent.
Visions of Murder, Coroner's Court and pursuit of
Homicidal Plumber throughout countryside flash across
my mind, and even have time to conduct brisk argument
with myself as to whether, under the circumstances, I ought
to Touch Nothing until the Police Come, or alternatively
whether I should snatch body down and apply Artificial
Respiration, when voice from corpse says huskily W'j'mind
pick'n up the stepladder pliz? Realise that his plight, far
from being fatal, is merely good old music-hall joke of
Fallen Ladder, and rescue him without comment as he is
scarlet with confusion.

Ask Where Plumber is? and Mate replies that Sgone
back t'fetch s'ming. (Really it was easier to understand him
during his silent period.) Remember that Plumbers
Forgetting Tools of their Trade is another well-known old
joke, what a traditionalist the man is, will he have us all
singing rousing Music-Hall Chorus before he has done
with us?

Feel that chances of entertaining conversation with Mate

146

are slight indeed, and leave him to amuse himself as best he can with New Tank, while I telephone unknown Americans and Maybelle.

Conversation with Maybelle is rendered difficult as she is evidently holding the baby, which screams loudly down the telephone. Suggest sympathetically that I have evidently chosen a bad moment to ring, and offer to try again later, but Maybelle replies blithely Oh no, the kids keep fussing but if I'll just hang on a minute, Junior will you get *away* from there, and goes on to say something else which I cannot hear at all due to renewed screechings from the baby and clearly audible argument from Junior. Entire picture very clear to me, and highly reminiscent of early days of James and Toby; am very sorry for Maybelle, but she is nonchalant and after sundry scufflings reduces her family to complete and alarming silence. Can only suppose she is sitting on the pair of them, but do not enquire too closely, and conversation can proceed. Why yes, Maybelle and Cliff would just love to come to coffee on Wednesday and meet unknown compatriots, how very very kind of me. Very nearly withdraw invitation when Maybelle adds thoughtfully that It's a Funny Thing how all her English friends always seem to think that the one thing Americans in England wish to do is to meet other Americans, but do not do so and we conclude with assurances from Maybelle that they will Surely Come, but that they May be Late. (Had rather taken that for granted anyway, have never yet known Maybelle and Cliff to arrive at any gathering less than an hour after appointed time.)

Telephone next to unknown American wife; she

answers in husky drawl that I feel must be Southern, and immediately envisage her as Scarlett O'Hara. She too is enchanted by extreme generosity of my invitation (feel rather guilty about this, in point of fact could hardly be offering less hospitality); she calls me by my Christian name from the start, which makes us feel old friends, and tells me all about her daughter, aged two, who has Sparts. Am sorry about Sparts, and ask what they are? Well Scarlett O'Hara doesn't quite know, she has sent for the doctor, she guesses it may be an Allergy. After this she goes on to tell me a great deal about Allergies suffered by herself, her husband, her mother and her father-in-law, about Allergies in general and drugs which do or do not cure them. (They seem to be an unduly sensitive lot.) Say bracingly that I expect it's Just Spots, and children often get these little upsets don't they? but this, as consolation, is no success at all, as Scarlett O'Hara evidently takes Motherhood and its responsibilities very seriously indeed, and delivers short lecture on how You Can't be Too Careful, and there's No Symptom without a Cause. Cannot escape conviction that she must be avid student of *Reader's Digest*, but however obtained her medical knowledge is certainly encyclopaedic, and I am quite unable to compete and listen respectfully to further expoundings of Childish Ailments, Virus Infections, and American methods of Paediatrics. Am eventually impelled to cut her short, what with lunch and the Plumber, and we ring off with final assurances that We Will Meet on Wednesday, Sparts permitting. (Wonder very much how Lee will get on with Scarlett O'Hara.)

*Tuesday, 6th*

Greta's turn to go to London. Much excitement. Wish she was taking the Aristocrat with her, but she says This Cannot Be (suggestion of dramatic emotional split here, but not at all, it is just that Aristocrat has used up quota of Days Off for months ahead and is to bend her proud hands to a little humble toil). James tells Greta bossily that she *must* go to Mme Tussaud's, as he wishes to be told all about Chamber of Horrors into which he was not allowed to penetrate. Greta looks alarmed but promises to go if she has time to this Mme Tussauds. (Am interested by remarkably different ways G and J have of pronouncing Mme T's name . . . but keep it out of my own remarks as I always have trouble with it myself.) Greta says she also intends to visit the Cathedral of St Paul, Number Ten Downing Street, The Tower of London and perhaps also see a Skiffle Group in a Coffee Bar. Equip her with maps and tell her that she must ask policemen how to get to places; own knowledge of London geography sketchy in extreme, but feel that she has set herself impossible programme. See her off, with some misgivings, from local station, and take children to school although it is not really my turn, but school is very near station.

Feel rather virtuous about this, but wish I hadn't later, as schoolmistress, Miss Young, catches sight of me and dashes out looking distraught and pleading. Children gallop in without a backward glance, but she detains me and says that Crisis has Arisen. Say apprehensively Oh dear, is it Toby? but she replies No no he's a darling, lovely boys both of them, no, what has happened is that her assistant Miss Bellamy has gone sick and probably won't be back for the concert and she can't get anyone to play the piano for it. Goodness, I say, stalling, I had no idea the concert was so soon. Miss Y says frenziedly that It has to be this month because so many of the children are going to be away in December, going to Switzerland. (Poor James and Toby; they *are* the church mice at this establishment. Hope lifelong complexes aren't being set up.) But do I, says Miss Y desperately, *do* I know *anyone* who could be persuaded to play just for the concert? She can manage herself for practises but on the Actual Day she daren't be tied to the piano (glimpse of unruly mob through classroom window gives point to this assertion). Am sorry for her and tell her that I will see if I can think of anyone. Miss Y says suspiciously that She doesn't suppose I play myself, do I? Do not really feel I can claim such musical prowess as my career stopped short in that direction somewhere about the Lower Fourth and *The Merry Peasant*. Still, we do have a piano and I do play songs for the children with one finger of the right hand and much banging of octaves with the left; tell her this, and offer my services if she can't find anyone better. She seems disposed to close with this at once, and I realise gloomily that I am committed unless I can find some local Myra Hess myself in the meantime. Hope James and Toby will not be too bitterly ashamed of me.

On homeward drive Ben says Bus, quite plainly, and I am triumphant, although well aware that achievement hardly constitutes a record in two-year-old prowess, and actually vehicle concerned was a lorry, but nonetheless

congratulate him warmly and he appears gratified and practises saying it all the way home.

Spend much of the day trying to remember how to play
the piano and practising sight-reading hymns in old *Songs of
Praise*. Mrs Parnell will probably think I am holding
Revivalist Meeting.

Greta returns earlier than expected in evening, having
got taxi from station at vast expense. Reprove her for this,
Lee or I could easily have fetched her if she had tele-
phoned, but she weeps and I suppose I have been too
severe, though really reproof was very mildly expressed. It
transpires however that she weeps not because of me, Ach
Gott Nein, it is that she has had Terrible Experience in
London. Heart sinks, what on earth can have happened,
take her into kitchen for soothing cup of tea and beg her to
Tell me all about it. (Am truly concerned, but regret to
observe that Lower Nature is asserting itself with avid
curiosity.)

It is in St Paul's Cathedral, says Greta weeping into her
teacup. (Surely a girl should be safe there if anywhere?)
Apparently not. She has, she says, been approached by
Catholic Priest while looking at statues, he has been So
Nice and has ask her to have tea with him. Fresh tears. And
what happened then, I ask, trying not to sound too eager.
Did she go? Ach yes she did, and he was then So Nasty. Oh
*dear*, how awful. Am deeply shocked at whole affair, no further details are immediately forthcoming and do not like to
press for them, anyway can well imagine. However further
questioning elicits fact that they did not actually *go out* of
teashop when Nastiness occurred, so it can't have been

The Worst in such a public place. Still, whole encounter has left poor G thoroughly shaken, and I do the best I can to console her.

(On later reflection I find entire story slightly unlikely; what would a Catholic Priest be doing in St Paul's Cathedral anyway . . . and of all people, if he was there at all, should have thought he was the least likely to approach innocent young girl with Nastiness. However my experience of Life is limited, as I am for ever discovering; don't think I shall make a very good novelist.)

Greta recovers before bedtime and joins us in the sitting-room, and tells us more about her day. She *did* manage to go to Mme Tussaud's, though not Skiffle Group, and has

found it interesting and very like similar exhibition in Hanover. (Nonsense, foreigners have nothing like Mme Tussaud's.) She has descended into Chamber of Horrors and was sad to see there Hitler. She agrees that he was Wicked Man but is his place not with Napoleon? Am inclined to think that there is something to be said for this argument, feel that International Unity is not best served by putting our late enemies in Chamber of Horrors, but can see Lee bristling at mere mention of Herr H in same breath as Napoleon, and change subject rapidly. (Should like, nonetheless, to ask him what he would think of seeing Sir Winston Churchill's effigy in similar position in Hanover establishment, or even Neville Chamberlain's.)

Tell them instead about epoch-making fact that Ben has Actually Spoken, and they are impressed.

*Wednesday, 7th*
Go into local town for dual purpose of Changing Library Books, thoroughly overdue, and buying proper coffee for Americans this evening. (Terrible hypocrisy this; why don't I give them Instant Coffee like we always have? Suspect that I am guilty of despised practice of Keeping up with the Joneses.)

Tweedy lady in Library is annoyed with me because books are late back, and speaks severely while everyone listens and looks at me reprovingly. Feel as though I am back at school, and apologise. It is Very Difficult, I say, because I find it almost impossible to remember when Library is Open. No excuses please, says Tweedy lady, You People from Your Village are all the same, it's always

You Lot who fail to return books. Well, please may I pay Fine, I ask, hoping to stop her before she gives me Five Hundred Lines to write. No, I may not. We don't have Fines System, says Tweedy Lady superbly, we prefer to rely on Publicspiritedness of Borrowers. (Very optimistic and tiresome of her, would much rather pay fine and avoid this public Stool of Repentance.)

Eventually make yet more abject apologies and creep away to shelves to choose fresh books. Cannot see anything whatever that I want to read, still less anything that will suit Lee, but can feel Tweedy Lady watching me with venom and hastily select C. S. Forester and Peter Cheyney for him, on grounds that even if he has read these particular ones already he'll never notice; and *Colette* and unknown female novelist for me, as *Colette* will make me feel sophisticated and Unknown looks as though it's about humble domestic affairs which will make me feel at home.

Tweedy lady eyes selection with scorn, obviously no better than she had expected, and bangs date stamp on them with vigour. Should very much like to tell her not to treat me so off-handedly as I am practically a Distinguished Writer and Broadcaster, but doubt if she would believe this (in which she would, of course, be entirely justified), and make hasty getaway, followed by bellowed injunction to Be Sure to bring this lot back in Good Time, please. Pretend I am out of earshot.

Go to superior grocer in pursuit of Good Coffee for Americans, and buy half a pound at hideous expense. Follow this up with insane purchases of Tinned Shrimps, Savoury Biscuits and Cream Cheese, with vague idea (engendered by Hollywood and glossy magazines) that this is the sort of thing Americans like to eat. Grocer seems surprised that this is all I want, and despatches me to Cash Desk with little chitty. Total shame descends on me here, as I find I have not got enough money (purse seemed very full when I left home, but it turns out to be all pennies). Make blushing apologies to glamour-girl at Cash Desk and say I will Be Back Later, and hurry away to Post Office to cash Family Allowance. (Am not at all sure that this is what Government gives me money for; can only hope they would approve of contribution to Anglo-American goodwill in lieu of shoe-repairs for Toby, which will have to wait yet another week).

Grocer, when I finally return and pay for purchases, is tolerant and agrees with me that Money Goes Nowhere these days. (Most of it, actually, as far as I am concerned, goes into his till; but perhaps he has his own problems.)

Wash hair in afternoon, decide as usual that I Need a Perm and that hair was very much easier to deal with before Mr Charles was so artistic with it. Also find it very difficult to get it dry, as Lee has decreed that in future we are to burn Only Coke in sitting-room fire, which is no doubt economical and patriotic measure, but results in small smoky slag-heap which gives off no heat whatsoever.

Point this out to him on his return. He is superior and says that it is Just that I don't know How to Manage It, and does masterful things with poker. Fire instantly goes out. Leave him to it, only hope that he will achieve some sort of cheerful glow before Americans arrive, as I do not wish to hear ever again how cold English houses are.

155

Scarlett O'Hara and husband arrive punctually in enormous car that takes up entire drive. (She *is* very like Scarlett O'Hara. Very small, very brunette, very glamorous. Or was S. O'H. a redhead?) Husband, introduced as Stooart, is tall and willowy with very short hair and unnatural air of being very much *cleaner* than any of the rest of us. Welcome both of them cordially and say optimistically Come in and get warm. (Fire is going again, strong smell of paraffin indicates that Lee has been having trouble, and room is Arctic.)

Scarlett and Stooart refuse sherry and cigarettes, looking slightly shocked, and I wonder what on earth we are going to talk about. (Am sorry to think that my conversational powers are entirely dependent on alcoholic stimulus, but such appears to be the case.) Scarlett, however, is not similarly inhibited, and tells us all about England. Many things, it appears, do not measure up to standards Back Home. The butchers' shops revolt her, the milk is not Homogenised and Tastes Strange, the hotel service is terrible and the Spoons are all the Wrong Size. Am very sorry about all these deficiencies, but can do little to remedy them except offer to explain the sizes of spoons, as she may need them when following English recipes. She refuses this offer, as she will not be requiring any English recipes. French yes; English no. Before I can spring to defence of much-maligned English cooking she goes on to complain that our system of money is incomprehensible to her, she can't think why we don't have cents and dollars, and No English Kitchen has a Refrigerator in it.

By this time am seriously tempted to take her and thrust her bodily into my own fridge, but am rescued by Stooart, who evidently feels that his wife is not being a complete social success. (Could this be something to do with undoubted fact that I am crimson in the face and Lee is scowling horribly?)

Stooart tells us all about Cultural Exchange, and is interesting. (Would be more interesting if Scarlett did not argue and interrupt quite so constantly.) Stooart and his colleagues are, it appears, engaged on something called a Comparative Survey of English Literatures, and I feel that this is in my own line of country and try to be intelligent. This is not entirely successful as Stooart not only knows very much more about American literature than I do, which is reasonable, but also appears to have read every word of every British author from Chaucer onwards, which obscurely annoys me. Do my best to keep up with him but he keeps telling me to Look at my Hardy, to Remember my Fielding and Consider my Meredith, and I have great difficulty in keeping up pretence that I am as familiar with these masters as I should like him to think I am. My attempts to introduce own favourites Jane Austen and Trollope are kindly but briefly dealt with, and when we find ourselves on Ezra Pound and Walt Whitman I decide that it is time I got the coffee.

Extra cups on tray remind me that Maybelle and Cliff are expected; but decide not to wait for them and proffer coffee and shrimp-and-cheese savouries. Apologise automatically for well-known fact that English coffee is not as good as American, but Scarlett, after an apprehensive sip, declares with rather offensive astonishment, that it's Not at Arl Bad; shrimp-and-cheese savouries however are less successful with her, as she only nibbles at the edge of one and then leaves it. (Wish I had had Toby's shoes mended instead of spending all that money.) Am mollified on this score by Stooart who is really making heroic efforts to redress his wife's tactlessness, and eats many with appreciation.

Scarlett leads the conversation round to Beauty-Parlours. Do I go to them? she asks, and adds, before I can answer, that she Guesses I don't. (Splendid repartee No I don't need to only occurs to me long after they have departed.) Beauty-parlours in this country, it appears, are very unsatisfactory. Just look, cries Scarlett, at her Hair. We all look, while she waves raven tresses in all directions. Think myself that it looks all right, though too long; but Scarlett has much to say about unfashionable style inflicted upon her by ignorant English hairdresser. And talking of style reminds her of difficulties she has in obtaining clothes to fit her in this country. She gazes piteously at Lee and invites him to Imagine, her waist is So Small she gets sent to the Juvenile Department. Lee looks unimpressed. Am myself less sympathetic than I should be, considering the fact that I have much the same trouble in the opposite direction. (*Outsize* department for Madam I think.) Anglo-American understanding not really flourishing, am thankful at this stage to hear Maybelle and Cliff arrive.

Am delighted to see them, give them remains of coffee and savouries, and conversation becomes domestic. Junior and the baby have apparently been giving trouble, but Maybelle is carefree about them and says Oh kids, they're terrible and she must be crazy to want more, but they plan to have Six. Am impressed by this, but Scarlett is shocked and takes us earnestly to task on our irresponsibility; Motherhood is to her in all its aspects a Sacred Trust and she feels herself that One is enough, as she can devote herself fully to the Child's Development. Feel that this is all far too idealistic to be successful, and that Scarlett's daughter is in for an awful childhood; but do not, of course, say so, and ask instead about progress of Spots? Long medical speech follows that none of us can stem; daughter has apparently been suffering from one ailment or another ever since she arrived in England, and in no time at all we are back on Unhygienic Shops and Strange Taste of Milk.

This subject lasts her, despite all our endeavours, until Stooart persuades her that it is Time they Went, and Scarlett agrees, looking harassed at the thought of returning to her onerous duties of Motherhood.

In farewell they both assure us that they have had a Swell Evening, and that it has been Wonderful to see our Lovely Home. Do not entirely believe them, but am only too glad to know that Scarlett is capable of expressing appreciation of anything.

After they have gone we spend pleasurable half-hour with Cliff and Maybelle, telling each other how much we disliked Scarlett and how sorry we are for Stooart. Maybelle says solemnly that we are Not to think All American Women are like that, and we assure her, truthfully, that we don't and we won't.

*Thursday, 8th*
Frightful inferiority complex instilled by Scarlett O'Hara and her unnatural waist leads me to decide quite definitely

to diet. (Fact that we have run out of bread is, no doubt, contributory factor.) Discovery that there is to be neither Toast *nor* Fried Bread is not well received by anyone at breakfast, despite fact that they have all already eaten enormous helpings of porridge, and Lee says wittily that he supposes this is what is known as a Skeleton Service? Retort that he is forever moaning about putting on weight himself, and that I must think about My Figure. James murmurs to himself, at this, Figure of Speech? and is manifestly surprised when everyone greets this as humorous, so that I realise that I must absolve him of ironic intent. Greta is confused by all this merriment and wishes to have Joke Explained to her. Do my best, with long speech about English Idiomatic Usage, but catch myself resorting to broken English such as she uses herself in order to make it all more intelligible to her. Cannot really feel that this is of much advantage to any of us, least of all to Ben, who is no doubt taking it all in. Further linguistic exposition is anyway impossible as children are going to be late for school and Toby has lost a gumboot, which he appears to regard as Unkind Blow of Fate rather than any fault of his own.

Rest of day continues to be haunted by spirit of Scarlett O'Hara. Devote much time to thinking up splendid repartees I should have made to her, and wishing I had told her about B.B.C., recent visit to publisher and other Cultured Aspects of my life. Further consideration of these matters finally cause me to sit down at writing-desk with rather unworthy motive of proving myself superior to her by Doing Some Writing.

Cannot think of anything whatever to write, but drag out Chapter One of book and re-read it, and quote to myself, probably incorrectly, *Ah what genius I had then.* Decide to write Chapter Two, but perhaps had better clean typewriter first. Little toothbrush affair for this operation is nowhere to be found. Search unavailingly for it in drawers of desk, and find instead small broken doll (doll? in *this* household?), old school Colt's Colours for netball, three kirbigrips and letter dated June 1938 addressed to Lee and apparently preserved with loving care. Open it unscrupulously in hopes of revelations about Lee's Past, but am disappointed to find that it is from his mother reminding him to Thank Aunt Alice for unspecified Birthday Present.

Put them all back where they came from, with mental resolve to clear out desk thoroughly one day, and try again to think about book. (*Dénouement* is quite clear in my mind, am dying to get on to that, but feel that Chapter Two is not the place for it; cannot help feeling that publisher, with best will in the world, is hardly likely to accept book with only three chapters in it.)

Try to remember eloquent flow of narrative which seemed so good in the bath last night, but it remains elusive; for no apparent reason, however, idea for Article presents itself which seems to me to be Funny; begin to write it down with great excitement, typewriter's spelling perfectly hysterical but never mind, can correct that later . . . am just getting well into my stride when nervous tap on door distracts me. Greta peers timorously round with many apologies for disturbing me, which makes me feel gratifyingly literary, and then tiptoes with dramatic caution into room and whispers Is it not time for Ben's walk? Yes, it is, I whisper back, would she be very kind and take him? (Why on earth am *I* whispering?) But yes, she hisses, she loves to take him, but *where is? where is?* Thought he was with her, spring up in concern and we seek him madly. (Little one oh little one! I am searching everywhere! . . . thank goodness the garden gate is shut.) Am rapidly getting into Maternal Frenzy and Greta is wringing her hands more madly than ever when Donald Duck noises from coal-shed give us a clue, and Ben is discovered, knee-deep in coke, looking like a small black minstrel. Greta clasps her hands over her heart hysterically and I am annoyed with both of them. Subsequent cleansing operations take so long that when I finally despatch them for walk it is practically lunchtime, and I abandon Witty Article in favour of potato-peeler and kitchen sink. (Still think Article was funny; shall try it out on Lee this evening and finish it if it makes him laugh.)

Toby on return from school is depressed, and tells me he is *not* to be a shepherd in School Play after all, owing to disagreement with Miss Young over Six Times Table, but has been demoted to taking part that he refers to as The Little Alf. (Sounds like character in a strip cartoon, this is going to be a very odd Nativity Play.) Ask for more information about The Little Alf, and he says impatiently that it's just one of the lot who stand in a Sammy-circle. Much deep thought enables me at length to understand this, but am not impressed with purity of Toby's vowel-sounds.

Give Lee unfinished Article to read in evening, and stand over him watching his face intently while he reads it. Stop him whenever I think he has got to a funny bit and ask indignantly why he isn't screaming with laughter. He says it is Very Difficult to Concentrate with me glowering at him like that, and if I would please go out of the room he will try again. Go and stand in hall and listen hopefully. He laughs quite distinctly, twice, and I am elated, but when I rejoin him he confesses that laughs were caused by eccentric spelling, and he thinks really it would be Better if I got on with my Book. Adds kindly that article is Quite Good, though not frightfully funny and seems surprised when I am offended. Well, I wanted his opinion didn't I? he asks reasonably; and pride compels me to keep to myself truthful reply that what I actually wanted was unstinted praise.

*Friday, 9th*

Countryside swathed in impenetrable fog. Everyone seems unreasonably astonished by this phenomenon, and B.B.C. and newspapers can talk of nothing else. Ask Lee if he thinks he can get the children to school and himself to work safely, but he scoffs at any suggestion of hazard and says the only thing that will stop him getting away is if those Perishing Children don't get a move on. Abandon wifely anxieties, and concentrate on hustling James and Toby into dufflecoats and gumboots and they disappear into the murk looking like gnomes. Hope I shall ever see any of them again.

Greta asserts that she would like to Bake a Cake, and I leave her to perusal of recipe-book while I deal with beds. (High time children had clean sheets, am as usual days behind on laundry schedule due to vagaries of weather.) Am just ruefully contemplating enormous tear in Toby's bottom sheet when loud scream from kitchen sends me hot-foot back to Greta again.

She is standing apparently rooted in horror gazing into the oven, from which quite indescribably horrid smell is issuing. Oh what is, what is, she wails. See, see, I have the oven on but nothing in, and now is *this*. Cannot imagine what it is all about, sight of G's blanched face and starting eyes very nearly cause me to begin babbling hysterically too without even investigating cause, but pull myself together and peer into evil-smelling oven. Am quite prepared to find anything, from very small Martians to part of decaying corpse, but in fact only discover mysterious glutinous red pool. Switch oven off with belated caution and pursue

researches more closely; small lump in midst of pool at last gives me a clue, as on removal it proves to be partially melted head of one of Toby's plastic soldiers. Remainder very very difficult to remove, and smell of melted plastic haunts kitchen for rest of morning. Am very brisk and bright with Greta about entire incident, as can otherwise foresee that she will spend all day reliving her astonishment and alarm with gusto, and suggest that we should take opportunity to Clean Oven thoroughly and Do the Walls while we are at it. She agrees with very modified enthusiasm, and we immerse ourselves.

Kitchen walls cover far larger area than I had hitherto realised, and Greta alleges that she Cannot put her head in oven to clean it as This Smell make her Sick, and that she

Cannot clamber on chairs to clean upper parts of walls as This make her Dizzy. With this limited assistance it is lunch-time before kitchen is finished, I am exhausted, and walls look exactly the same as ever.

After lunch decide that I May as well Make a Job of it, and scrub floor. Ben is recalcitrant about having his Rest, but leave Greta to deal with him while I perform final sloshings and splashings. Bright lady on B.B.C. chooses this moment to urge me to Lie Down and Relax. Refuse utterly to do so whereupon she repeats, more brightly than ever, Come on now, just Lie down on the floor and Relax. Regard waste of waters surrounding me with gloom, and switch Bright Lady off.

Later, state of Toby's sheet, and indeed most of the linen, sends me to sit at sewing-machine. Yet another very uncongenial activity, and one at which I am very bad, but still am grateful that it is more comfortable and less ungainly occupation than crawling about kitchen floor in a puddle. Am just performing ritual of Sides-to-Middling Toby's torn sheet when Susan arrives, looking very County in camel-hair coat and brogues. Welcome her in and am rather gratified at being for once discovered doing something comparatively ladylike, ask if she Minds if I Carry On, and she says No no, do, and seems impressed. Return to horrible sewing-machine saying merrily *Stitch stitch stitch*, *In poverty hunger and dirt*, but this rather a mistake as Susan looks slightly embarrassed and I don't think recognises that I am (in my cultured way) simply Quoting. (Culture not really very impressive now I come to think of it. Am very uncertain about context of quotation, only know it because it came into a Crossword Puzzle recently.)

Abandon erudition and ask her What brings her out in this awful fog? Oh says Susan, she had to exercise Biddy. Biddy is minute black dog, which is now revealed cowering under camel-hair coat. (Feel very sorry for the poor thing, which would obviously be far happier sitting by the fire at home; also think it looks suspiciously dry for one who has been exercised in foggy weather, would be prepared to bet that Susan has in fact carried it every step of the way.) Make friendly gestures towards Biddy, to which she replies by sneering slightly and averting her head, while Susan tells me all about her breeding, virtues, and intelligence. Listen to what I consider a reasonable amount of this, and then interrupt with offer of Cup of Tea. Wish afterwards that I hadn't, as Susan evidently considers this rather Common, and says Good Gracious no, not at this hour. What she really wanted to ask me was, What about coming to a Political Meeting with her? Isn't it about time I took an intelligent interest in These Things? Tell her indignantly that I *do* take a perfectly intelligent interest, and that in fact I will defend to the death my right to be a Floating Voter. She brushes this aside and says Oh yes, she knows all about *that*, but really I ought to come and listen to The Member, after all, ha ha ha, he might convert me to the Right Side. Feel instant inclination to become ardent Socialist (had better not tell Lee this), and say firmly but apologetically that I will *not* come to Political Meeting, at which Susan is disappointed in me and is disposed to argue. Arrival of Ben however averts actual outright quarrel, he and Biddy exchange friendly overtures, and I do some more machining of Toby's sheet. (Sheet is really remarkably grubby. Would have washed it before proceeding with mending operations had I known Susan was going to supervise the latter.) Just as I am finishing seam she looks at it with close attention and asks in surprise if I Always do it That Way? What, Sides-to-middling? I ask grandly; Yes, always. Oh, says Susan in reply. Then why am I middle-to-middling it? Discover that that is indeed what I have been doing, entire afternoon's efforts wasted and am not pleased. Susan on the other hand appears to find it entertaining, and takes herself off, clasping Biddy in her arms, and saying There I am you see, and Don't I think I'd be better employed taking an interest in Political Affairs than doing That Sort of Thing? Cannot unfortunately think of a telling reply, and see her off into the fog in indignant silence.

Nevertheless reflect afterwards that if indifferent abilities with sewing-machine and needle are primary qualities required in Political Life, the sooner I take it up the better.

James and Toby return late due to fog, and have much to say about super drive home in wizard Jaguar belonging to Billy's Father. (Local butcher.) Cut it all short ruthlessly in order to expostulate with Toby about Plastic Soldiers left in Oven. He relates long history of campaign which led to soldiers being secreted in this particular *cache*, which was apparently new and splendid tactical move in complicated miniature war which perpetually accompanies Toby's life. At the end of recital he says anxiously that he hopes I haven't *moved* them? and I have to confess that I haven't so much Moved Them as Liquidated Them, at which he becomes very agitated indeed and takes a long time to calm down. Final word on the subject is to beg me in future to Look Carefully in the oven before I switch it on, and to tell Greta to do the same. No other way of avoiding future similar tragedies apparently occurs to him.

*Saturday, 10th*
Fog still with us, B.B.C. still unable to think about anything else, least of all apparently whether or not I am to do broadcast. Lee takes morning off and occupies himself stripping old wallpaper off dining-room walls, with assistance of children. Ask whether we oughtn't to put dust sheets on furniture or clear the room or something? but Lee begs me not to interfere and continues to shower shreds of paper and chunks of crumbling plaster all over furniture and carpet. Suppose he knows what he is doing, but am myself unable to share his complacency, it looks to me as though existing paper was the only thing that was holding the walls upright. Toby, working with unprecedented zeal over by window, pulls off enormous swathe of paper and says Gosh look it's *black*. (Black wallpaper?) Lee exclaims with horror and says Leave that alone its Damp-proof, but Toby is far too wound up to stop and continues to peel it off by the yard. Wonder without much hope whether entire collapse of dining-room due to over-enthusiastic amateur decorating will be paid for by Insurance, and leave them to it.

Lady E-A's tea-party in afternoon. Am as usual unable to find anything fit to wear, cannot understand why my wardrobe is overflowing with clothes which are (*a*) unfit for any occasion whatsoever, (*b*) downright nasty, and (*c*) impossible to wear out. Suppose I must have chosen them myself at some time, but cannot think *why*. Can only suppose that Susan and Ruth are right about my having No Dress Sense. Finally struggle into tweed coat-and-skirt which is too tight and does not suit me, but has, I hope, County touch suitable for Lady E-A's Stately Home, and put children into clean clothes from head to foot. Am not at all sure that we shall look as though we have come Just as we Are, as promised, but Lee looks like redressing balance as he declares that old flannel trousers and sports coat will be perfectly adequate. My suggestion that he might at least comb some of the plaster out of his hair is ungratefully received as Just another example of Officious Nagging and he very nearly refuses to do it at all. (Nevertheless, observe that he *does* do it, and with considerable care. Cannot help feeling that nagging, though unattractive, is sometimes unavoidable in family life.)

*En route* for Stately Home deliver strong lecture to children about necessity for behaving well, observing their table manners, answering when they are spoken to, and, with visions of priceless *objets-d'art* all over the place, Not Touching Anything. Add, for Toby's benefit, that If I kick him under the table he is to think what he is doing wrong, *not* say Why Are You Kicking Me? Cannot myself think of any more nerve-wracking occasion than taking children to tea at home of rich elderly childless people.

Am, as so often before, quite wrong, as tea party is almost unmitigated success. Lady E-A greets us effusively (hair obviously newly done, it is positively Mediterranean blue and startling), and leads us well out of harm's way into small sitting-room where table is laden with all J and T's favourite foods. Lady E-A begs them to Sit Down and Make a Start while she makes tea, at which James and Toby settle down to systematic clearance of every plate in sight, with every appearance of unalloyed bliss. Am much impressed with our hostess's skill and forethought, though less so when I watch her making tea, which is an operation with which she appears to be unfamiliar. (Does not heat teapot, and allows minutes to elapse between switching electric kettle off and pouring water into pot . . . can only suppose this rite is normally performed by minions or perhaps Aristocrat; wonder if they have been hidden away for their sake or ours?)

Lady E-A's husband arrives at this stage, enormous man in leggings always referred to as S'Robert. He is stone-deaf, and does not speak, but rectifies this ommission with tremendous hearty laughs at intervals, which give general impression of *bonhomie* without actually requiring an answer. He and Ben take great fancy to each other, as Ben cannot speak and S'Robert could not hear him if he did, with result that each appears at last to have found someone who Really Understands Him, and they remain glued to one another for the greater part of the afternoon.

Children are too busy eating to misbehave much at tea, and am just assuring Lady E-A that I *do* give them plenty to eat at home, when Lee startles everyone considerably by falling off his chair and landing flat on his back on the floor with his legs in the air like a music-hall comic. Even Lady E-A's high-bred manners cannot wholly ignore this misfortune, we all exclaim and he gets up covered in confusion

and full of apologies, and to all our astonished enquiries can only repeat No he doesn't know why it happened, Yes, he is quite all right, and he is very sorry, and resumes his seat with considerable embarrassment. Feel very sympathetic but cannot think what Correct Social Gambit can possibly be after such an unusual misfortune, but am saved from further worry by James, who asks in awed tones, What will Mummy say to You on the way home? at which everybody laughs gratefully, including the uncomprehending but willing Ben and S'Robert.

After this *contretemps* children evidently feel that family honour is at stake, and behave in exemplary fashion, at which I am gratified and Lady E-A obviously impressed. (Feel nevertheless that it is perhaps unconventional way of obtaining Good Manners, and hope Lee will not see fit to make habit of it.)

After tea we play Charades, in which Lady E-A and Lee distinguish themselves but I do not, and children score immense success with two-syllabled word, *Beer*, followed by *Row*, which they act with zest and mystify everybody until they reveal that word is *Bureau*.

Fog thicker than ever, and have much difficulty in getting home, but all are agreed that It was Well Worth It. Lee goes so far as to press me to admit that Lady E-A is really Very Nice, and I admit freely that she is excellent hostess, charming to children and amiable and sprightly to a remarkable degree, but that I am unable to escape conviction that she Does not Like Me. Lee does not contradict this, rather to my indignation, and I am left feeling that this is extraordinary and incomprehensible state of affairs.

*Sunday, 11th*

Fog fortunately cleared at last, and I take Toby to watch British Legion and Girl Guides performing Armistice Day ceremonies at War Memorial, and subsequently to Church. He asks many pertinent questions in a loud voice, and I am thankful that I have begged Greta to stay at home with James, who is coughing, as she would rightly dislike very much his belligerent reaction to any mention of our late enemies.

During Two-minutes-Silence am quite unable to concentrate as T apparently develops uncontrollable itch, and contorts himself frenziedly to get at it, until I obtain what I hope is an unobtrusive Half-Nelson on him. Patriotism of both of us severely strained.

Sermon, for which he insists on staying, is long and orotund, and Toby listens to it with passionate attention. (More than can be said for Mrs Parnell, whom I can see over to my right, nodding peacefully.) Preacher is much addicted to rhetorical questions, and is inspired at one stage to assert that We can't live with One Foot in the Grave, can we? which Toby receives as a good joke and laughs heartily, and agrees (aloud) No of course we can't. Heads of Girl Guides all swivel in our direction, and I try to look as though it wasn't us. Preacher goes on to say sententiously that Life is like a Game of Snakes and Ladders, at which Toby leaps to his feet excitedly and says We've got that at home, at which I blush and tell him to Hush, and Girl Guides all swivel more fascinatedly than ever. Preacher's final effort, which brings my heart into my mouth, is to say Suppose I were to ask you a Riddle . . . but fortunately before actually asking it he evidently remembers presence of Toby and interpolates hastily that he does not expect any of us to provide answer here and now. Can feel Toby relaxing disappointedly, and am thankful when sermon draws to a close and we all sing National Anthem and go home.

Dining-room now resembles Primitive Cave rather than habitation of civilised human beings, we shall evidently have to resign ourselves to eating in the kitchen for a long time yet, Gracious Living still a long way off. Lee and James however are delighted with themselves and urge us to observe what a lot they have done. Lee goes as far as to say that there's Not Much More to do Now, only the Actual Papering, which sounds to me optimistic in the extreme, and Greta emerges from under large pile of torn paper to tell me about progress of James' cough (which I can hear for myself is flourishing), and that she Has Herself sore throat, and sniffs to prove it.

*Monday, 12th*
James' cold too heavy for him to go to school but not bad enough to justify bed. He accordingly remains at home and very kindly offers to Help me, which he does by following me about the house three inches behind my heels, so that I tread on him every time I turn round. He appears to bear no malice at this and remains impervious to my suggestions that he should Go and sit by the fire with a Book, or Make something with Meccano. (Why do my children never *do* anything?) Finally decide that, devoted mother though I may be, I cannot stand his sniffing *one minute longer*, and tell him to Go and Finish stripping

dining-room wallpaper for Daddy, and he retires looking mildly hurt.

Conscience smites me about this later, and I follow him, to discover that he is not stripping wallpaper at all, but is sitting on the table reading *Songs of Praise*. This reminds me of forthcoming School Concert, and I ask him to tell me which carols I am likely to be called upon to play. He seems totally ignorant on the subject, but we pick out the most likely ones and perform rather uncertain recital. Am very much put-about by Four Flats, and by chords in the left hand which all seem to require eight fingers and span of at least two octaves, but cover up deficiencies as best I can with much use of loud pedal, and we struggle on through *Thus Spake the Sherriff and Forthwith*. James, despite many interruptions for sniffs and coughs, sings tunefully, and I am impressed and ask him whether he would like to be a Choirboy? (Think he would look well in a surplice, and

knowledge of Aunt Elizabeth's beneficence does not deter me from thinking optimistically about Choral Scholarships.) J however is bleak about this and says curtly that he would Rather be a Cowboy; abandon vision of angelic-voiced soloist in Magdalen College Chapel, and we pursue vagaries of *The First Nowell*. Rather rash attempt on my part to sing descant to this not a success, and James' version, *They went, To seek for a King who was there in a Tent*, distracts me badly. Ask him if he thinks my accompaniments will be adequate for Concert, and he says doubtfully that he supposes so, but Miss Bellamy plays Much Quicker than I do. Had better put in some intensive practice.

Weather has become Arctic; had, as usual, forgotten how nasty Winter in the Country was, and am torn between inclination to put on every warm undergarment I possess and conviction that I had better keep something in reserve for further horrors which no doubt are in store for January.

Ruth rings up to ask What about the B.B.C.? Not a word, I tell her resentfully, I think they have forgotten all about me. Ruth asserts that This won't do, and I'd better write to Miss Appleyard. Feel that this is overbold sugges- tion and tell her that I couldn't Possibly. Nonsense, says Ruth briskly, *she* would. (Daresay she would, and get away with it. She is established writer and broadcaster and has every right to address B.B.C. authorities in very different tones from those which I feel more becoming to me.)

Change subject to perennially fruitful one of Cold Weather. Ruth groans dramatically and says She Can't *Tell* me how bitter her house is, and proceeds to do so at some length. Am sympathetic, but point out that Wearing enough clothes is the thing, and that I have found that Two Pairs of Knickers make All the Difference. Ruth is horrified by this and says with heavy sarcasm that she Supposes I'll say I wear Two Vests next? Well, I reply, actually I do, often, am only not doing so yet because I am saving that for even colder weather ahead. Ruth reacts to this confession with renewed passion (at least she must be getting nice and warm), and says Really I am *impossible*, how do I expect to Have a Figure with all that clutter? My Bust-Line will be quite obscured. (Cannot think why she doesn't write for women's magazines.) Assure her that my bust-line is *better* obscured, and she sighs a good deal and says that I am *Hopeless*; am depressed, but unconverted.

Remainder of day spent in unsuccessful attempts to get washing dry.

Lee says kindly that he will Make me a Spin Dryer. Try to be grateful about this offer, but would very much rather save up for a real one while he gets on with the dining-room. Offer to help him with the latter, but he says he is Sick and Tired of stripping wallpaper, and isn't going to do any more. But we can't leave it like *this* can we? I say, looking at wall surfaces which look more like Primitive Caves than ever. (Should never be surprised to descry faint outlines of Early Neolithic drawings.) Lee says hardily Yes we can, he will put new wallpaper on tomorrow, Bold Stripes will cover that up perfectly well, it's great nonsense about having to strip walls completely. (Very different from his original sentiments. All yesterday's demolition-work presumably wasted if he is right.) Decide not to argue, and merely ask Why not get on with it Now? to which he replies with very unconvincing show of regret that there is nothing he'd like better but unfortunately we haven't any paste. Think that chances of Dramatic Society being surprised by changed aspect of dining-room at next rehearsal are strong indeed, though perhaps not in the way originally intended.

*Tuesday, 13th*

James' cold better, but Toby has it, and is coughing with gusto, Greta has it and is sniffing, and Ben has it and would be slightly less revolting if he *did* sniff. Leave them all to paper handkerchiefs and self-pity and take myself off to Dentist. (Find myself welcoming this expedition as positive relief from conditions prevailing at home. This proves however to be purely temporary and illusory state of affairs, as am in usual state of craven terror by the time I arrive in contemporary waiting-room.)

. Dentist, more Beethoven-like than ever, is brisk with me, and finds much to be done. Usual horrors of drilling, spitting, opening wider and vicious probing follow, large lumps of tooth fall about freely, and insult is added to injury by sudden remembrance that This is all going to Cost me a Pound. Almost wish I were pregnant again, as this state, though inconvenient in many ways, would at least permit me to receive ministrations of Beethoven for nothing. This reflection leads me to think of Grantly Dick-Read and his optimistic theories, and Relaxation, supposed to be so helpful in combatting discomfort. Try it out (though not, naturally, in position advocated for Expectant Mothers), and find it surprisingly effective, for the few seconds during which I am able to achieve it. Also have recourse to habitual method of Keeping My Mind off my Teeth, which is custom, evolved by me in early childhood, of running through all the Worst Words I know. (Selection these days quite impressive, should never dream of using any of them, but feel quite childishly elated at knowing such wickedness.) Feel that one way and another I am being distinctly successful in efforts to ignore Beethoven's activities, but am considerably startled when he suddenly breaks long silence in order to tell me slightly indelicate story. Story is actually very funny, would laugh heartily if I had the use of my mouth, but am nonetheless very suspicious as to why he should suddenly have decided that I was suitable audience for it, have thoroughly uneasy feeling that he may be Telepathic, and try hastily to switch mind to purer matters. (B.B.C. too depressing and current Premium Bond excitement not due yet, and funny article not funny at all; perhaps I could write it all over again quite ordinarily and then go through it afterwards Putting in Witty Bits? Have a notion that Real Writers don't do things that way.) Abandon efforts at coherent thought, and between twinges of purest agony (does he really have to drill right *on* the nerve?) practise exercise which is supposed to be Good for the Tummy Muscles. This may or may not have desired effect on Figure, but at least sees me through to end of session without actually bursting into loud screams.

Beethoven ushers me kindly out, and disdains Pound as he says that there is still A Lot to be Done. Make further appointments and spend most of Pound on the way home on medicaments for sniffing household.

## Wednesday, 14th

Everybody quite healthy again except me. I have a cold. Sniffing and coughing appear in quite a different light when it is me doing them, and am not pleased when Lee begs me unsympathetically to Use a Handkerchief or Go to Bed.

## Thursday, 15th

Cold very severe indeed, am not at all sure that it is not pneumonia. Stay in bed and leave everything to Greta and she rushes about tirelessly, and comes in at five-minute intervals to ask permission or advice on every detail of houschold management. Ben spends greater part of day with me, climbs affectionately all over bed and tears page out of library book while I am not looking. (Hope Selotape repairs will escape Tweedy Lady's eye.) Trappism clearly on the way out, as he conducts long monologue consisting of the word *Bus*, repeated with many varied and interesting inflections, alternated by urgent requests for Potty, with which I unwillingly deal, though delighted at his progress in this direction.

James and Toby very kindly come and keep me company after school and conduct animated argument about well-known historical figure Sir Hyde Park. Toby very knowledgeable about him, sweeps aside my pedantic doubts, and assures me that he was Famous Admiral in Nelson's time. Accept this for the sake of peace, knowing well that it is waste of time to argue with Toby about anything appertaining to Nelson, on whose life and times he is self-constituted authority, and instead beg James to Leave my reading-lamp Alone. He does not do so, and

Sir Hyde Park

reading-lamp presently falls heavily to the ground (entirely of its own volition according to James) and goes out.

Lee later mends it with some difficulty and tells me I

Look Better. Contradict him indignantly and tell him at some length how bad my cold is, much worse than anyone else's, and retail symptoms in some detail. He is unimpressed by my graphic description of how my sinuses feel, and tells me that That is Exactly the way all his Neurotic Women Patients describe their ailments. Am considerably dashed by this, and he proceeds most unfairly to Take my Temperature, which, I am not at all pleased to learn, is Well Below Normal. Resign myself to the fact that I am Not Ill at All, and decide to get up tomorrow.

Final touch of shame is added to my *malade imaginaire* when Lee says He may as well take his own temperature while he's at it. Ask Why? and he says he hasn't been feeling very well all day, perhaps I hadn't noticed that he has this cold too? No, I hadn't, and am ungraciously disposed not to believe it until he triumphantly proves it by discovering that *his* temperature is Just Over a Hundred.

Think thermometer must be out of order.

*Friday, 16th*
Cold sufficiently modified to allow me to resume normal life. This indeed proves essential, as Lee remains huddled under bedclothes, refuses to get up even to shave and says he thinks he is going to die. Remove thermometer from him, as he seems disposed to take his temperature every fifteen minutes, and to my offer of Breakfast in Bed only groans hollowly. Yesterday's activities have moreover caused Greta to suffer a relapse, and she is wan and droopy at breakfast and grateful when I suggest she had better go to bed too.

Just as I am issuing usual cottage-pies and blanc-manges to children for school lunch, James says brightly that he thought it was today he was due at the Eye-hospital for check-up? Hasty reference to desk-diary reveals that this is all too true, and that we shall have to be very speedy indeed if he is not to be late for his appointment. Toby says excitedly Can he come too? and unwillingly decide that he had better do so, if only to look after Ben while James and I are immured in Eye Department. Pile them into the car and drive away, leaving Greta and Lee both in bed. (Am slightly perturbed as to propriety of this state of affairs, and am inclined to ribald reflections as to what Mrs Parnell's reactions would be should she learn of it. No doubt she will. However, cannot help thinking that should she ever actually *see* Lee in bed with his cold, unshaven and huddled to the eyes in old ski-ing sweater, she would realise that chances of his figuring in really dramatic scandal were remote in the extreme.)

On arrival at Eye Hospital leave Toby in charge of Ben in the car, equip him with toys and toffees which he is to ration out in order to pass the time, assure him that We Shan't be Long anyway, and escort James to all-too-familiar Outpatients waiting-hall.

Painted Lady at reception-desk greets us without enthusiasm, waves away my explanations as to Why we are Late, motions us to sit down on bench without so much as glancing at us, and resumes muttered conversation with Assistant Painted Lady.

Time passes. Glamorous orthoptic young women bustle to and fro, other patients are called away and dealt with,

James becomes increasingly restless, and I evolve bad joke about Outpatients and Impatients. Try it out on James and he does not think it funny, but continues to kick bench and work away at Loose Tooth. Benches very hard and uncomfortable, apparently designed for use of deformed midgets, and no magazines or comics in sight. Write strong letter, full of constructive criticism, to Local Hospital Board, but only, unfortunately, in my head; am only too well aware that I should never have courage to do so in actual fact. Outpatient next to James, elderly lady, has quite frightful cough which she emits more or less continuously in very unhygienic fashion. Wonder if she is in the wrong department; feel sure she should be Chests, and very nearly tell her so until she turns towards me and I observe that she has most distressing squint. Despite cough and squint however she is amiable and says Dretful, in'it dear. Agree wholeheartedly, and James suddenly electrifies everyone by at last wrenching Loose Tooth from his head and waving it about with much excitement, bleeding freely the while.

All outpatients are indulgent and interested and offer much advice. Chorus of voices tells him to Lie Down, to Put his Head between his Knees, to put Tooth under his Pillow, to Rinse his Mouth Out, to Swallow the Blood, *Not* to Swallow the Blood, and to Leave Tooth for the Fairies Tonight. (This last suggestion is fortunately unheard by James, as he has strong and cynical views on Fairies.) Painted Lady and Assistant raise their heads from private discussion, and look disapproving at general excitement, but am nevertheless sufficiently brave to approach them and ask Where James could get a drink of Water? Painted

Lady turns from me in disgust, and Assistant points silently to large clear notice which says affectedly: *To The Toilets*. Say nervously Oh how silly I am, and Assistant shrugs with pitying smile which makes it very clear that she is in wholehearted agreement with this sentiment.

After mopping-up operations life in waiting-hall resumes more or less unbroken calm; keep telling James that it must be our turn soon, but it never is (can we be being penalised for being Rowdy Element?), and even cough-and-squint is presently told to Come Along Now, which she does with many a pitying backward glance at us.

Wonder nervously how Toby is getting on with Ben, and am just about to go and find out when James creates further disturbance by dropping newly extracted tooth on floor. Other outpatients much less sympathetic at this renewed disturbance, indeed feel that they are becoming positively hostile when James crawls under all their legs in course of his frantic seekings. Beg him to Come up and Leave it, very nearly add in desperation that I will Get Him Another (remarkably impracticable suggestion, as I fortunately realise before actually committing myself to it), but he refuses absolutely to abandon search and in the event his troubles are rewarded, as he emerges triumphantly clutching Tooth, now very dusty.

Painted Lady not pleased with this further outbreak of Rowdyism. (Perhaps she'll let us have our turn soon, if only to get rid of us?)

General attention is now riveted on us, wish very much that we could go away and never be seen again, but this is impossible, and can only try to look detached and unembarrassed. This fond hope is instantly frustrated by appearance in doorway of small tousled figure, covered in toffee-stains from head to foot, saying penetratingly Where is My Mother? I beckon and hiss at him frantically, everyone looks accusingly at me, and Toby sights me and continues plaintively Aren't you *ever* coming? Reassure him and say We won't be long now, I think it's our turn next (only hope this is true), and Toby, still lurking on threshold, exhibits horrified amazement and bellows Haven't you even been *seen* yet, I thought James must be having another *operation*. Outpatients show tendency to laugh sympathetically, Painted Lady looks apprehensive of incipient mutiny, and occupies herself with heap of Files. (Probably postponing our appointment for a further hour or so.) Finally persuade Toby to go back and collect Ben, feeling that I cannot in fairness leave them immured in car any longer, and that if I go out to pacify them I shall inevitably miss long-awaited moment of James' summons.

By the time this does actually occur entire department has had more than enough of all of us, and I of them.

Session with eye-doctor is by contrast brief in the extreme. Not Professor who did James' operation at all, but sombre stranger who deals briskly with James and has nothing constructive to say except that Operation has been Successful, which I already know, and that I am to make another appointment on my way out. Obviously expects us, after this, to go respectfully away, but I am rebellious and say that we have had a Very Long Wait, and were anyway expecting to see the Professor. Sombre stranger says irritably, Yes, Well, *everyone's* had a long wait today (*he* hasn't), and that the Professor is away, but may be able to see us next time. Quite unusual excess of moral courage descends on me at this and I tell him defiantly that I will *not* make further appointment with Outpatients Secretary, I cannot afford to spend all this time waiting about, and I will get my husband to ring the Professor direct. Sombre stranger is astonished at my temerity (so am I), becomes much more cordial and treats us for the first time as though we were human beings, purely on grounds, apparently, that he now realises that my husband is a colleague. Sweep out rather grandly feeling that I Have Won; but am not proud of having pulled even this very small string in order to obtain civil attention, and think it very regrettable that it should be either necessary or effective to do so.

On return home for very belated lunch, discover that Greta has recovered and is eating cold cottage-pie in the kitchen, Lee is asleep, and Christmas parcels have arrived from New Zealand, which jolts me into horrid realisation that once again I have forgotten to despatch our offerings there and it is now too late for anything except Air Mail.

*Saturday, 17th*
Weather very erratic. B.B.C. assures me at breakfast-time that Temperatures are going to continue Below Average for time of Year; do not know what Average is, but assume they mean that it is going to be perishing and put boys and self into quantities of thick sweaters. Sun immediately comes out and we are all too hot.

Lee, on being reminded that we are due at Party at Susan's this evening, says He is Better, and gets up, but very nearly goes back to bed on sight of Caves of Lascaux in dining-room. Am not surprised when he says he is Not Strong Enough to do papering today, but feel that his alternative occupation of Making Bonfire in garden will be hardly less exhausting.

Feel sure that Susan's party will be very sophisticated affair, cannot think what to wear, choice lies between flowery taffeta that looks like child's party-frock on a large scale, and Old Black. Settle for Old Black, as being more sophisticated, and anyway Taffeta has split under one arm that I have been putting off mending for months.

Lee also gives much thought to his appearance, says several times that he wishes he had Another Suit, and Why do I never send his Ties to the Cleaners? Toby, on hearing this, kindly proffers bright yellow tie of his own with Davy Crockett all over it, and says that Daddy may borrow it. (Davy Crockett bears traces of several recent birthday parties and has well-chewed end.) Lee declines, very kindly, but Davy Crockett nevertheless appears, carefully laid out on his bed, when he finally goes to change.

Old Black looks horrible, older and blacker than ever. Do my best to brighten it up with Paste Brooch and Earrings, the latter very painful, but am regretfully forced to conclusion that I look like a Barmaid. Remove Paste trinkets, and look like third-rate saleswoman. Put them on again; would rather be a barmaid.

Lee looks very groomed and suave and does me credit. Feel faint twinge of shame however when he points out complacently How well this Drip-Dry Shirt has come up Without Any Ironing.

Susan's house surrounded by opulent cars. Party is evidently large and grand, elegant drawing-room is crowded with people I have never seen before, but am relieved to observe that every other woman in sight is also wearing black. This makes me feel fashionable though cannot escape conviction that general impression is depressingly funereal.

Susan greets us effusively, and hisses Isn't it Wonderful, Anna Farthingale is here, Lady E-A brought her. (Name Anna Farthingale very familiar indeed, know perfectly well that she is Famous Woman of Our Time, a Dame and a Name and a positively Legendary Figure; but when Lee hisses at me Who is she and What does she Do, am quite unable to remember.)

Presence of A. F. undoubtedly lends tone to the party, everyone's conversation is unusually cultured, find myself very soon involved in deep discussion on *Dr Zhivago* with slender young man with eyelashes. He has much to say, but so, owing to Susan's excellent cocktails, have I. Neither of us is so tactless as to ask the other outright if they have Actually Read Dr Z, which in my case is just as well, and I suspect in Eyelashes' too. Nonetheless we both quote the critics and feel that we are sustaining the right note.

Lady E-A presently materialises, whisks me away from Eyelashes (am really quite pleased about this as had some time ago reached point of saying my Last Word on Dr Z though Eyelashes undoubtedly full of charm), and says Come along dear, I want you to meet Anna Farthingale. Am immediately filled with horror and say No no, please not, I really only want to Look at her from a Distance; but Lady E-A forges ahead unheeding and I can only follow her. We reach sofa on which A. F. is enthroned holding Audience. Very remarkable and impressive sight, in black like the rest of us, but flowing draperies, strings of amber and cascades of diamonds render whole effect very different from barmaid-saleswoman *motif*: Enormous hat of witch-like proportions shades her white, clever, and thoroughly alarming face, and from beneath its shadow piercing eyes look at me and Know All. (Should give a great deal to turn and run at this stage. At least I could tell my grand-children that I Actually Saw Anna Farthingale.) Cannot however do so, and Lady E-A presents me. (*Wish* I could remember particular form of A. F.'s distinguished activities.)

Pale bejewelled hand waves me graciously to sit on the sofa beside it. Do so with singular lack of elegance, Lady E-A meanly melts away, and we are surrounded by small oasis of respectful silence. Anna F. bends her head graciously towards me and waits. Am totally unable to think of any-thing whatsoever to say, and can only gaze back at her with profound horror, that I hope she will mistake for speechless adoration. Evidently she does, as she allows it to go on for hours and hours, while intelligent or even coherent speech recedes further and further from me. At length A. F. appar-ently decides that I have had my ration of silent devotion and asks hollowly Am I a Reporter? (She must think I am an astonishingly poor one.) Reply hoarsely No I am Not. This concludes my scintillating contribution to Conversations with the Great, and we relapse again into silent communion. By this time am almost as sorry for A. F. as I am for myself, cannot escape suspicion that she is accustomed to brighter exchanges than this, but remain inexplicably rooted to Audience Sofa. Am very grateful indeed when Susan comes to the rescue and says that I Mustn't monopolise the Guest of the Evening Any Longer (a pleasing euphemism), and leads me away.

She and Lee are kind, give me several more drinks, and have the good feeling not to ask what A. F. and I talked about.

Cultural note is allowed to lapse temporarily and I tell Susan about Toby's hero Sir Hyde Park, and she is amused. This is also new to Lee, and he forgets customary disapproval of my tendency to Talk About the Children, and laughs heartily. After some thought he goes so far as to pronounce that the Issue seems Confused, which, once I see it, strikes me as witty, and am impressed; though Lee points out later that he does not think it necessary for me to be quite so *surprised* when he makes a joke.

Lady in what looks like Uncut Moquette surges up to me. Cannot remember her name, but face is familiar, she lives in neighbouring village, we have been introduced on several occasions, and my only impression of her is that she made *no* impression on me nor I on her. She is however surprisingly effusive, and explains this quite uninhibitedly by saying that she'd no idea I was so *interesting*. Nor had I, what can she mean? (She certainly cannot have witnessed my reccnt skirmish with Anna F.) Wait for further elucidation, and she goes on to refer to my Broadcasting and my Writing, about which, it appears, Ruth has just been telling her. (Cannot avoid suspicion that Ruth has been allowing her story-teller's imagination to run away with her, but am flattered nevertheless and think it is generous of Ruth.)

Endeavour to reply deprecatingly that I Haven't Done Much Yet, but am not above hoping that Uncut Moquette will think that this is merely modest understatement. She evidently does, as she goes on to make wholly fantastic suggestion that it would be So Nice if I were to come and Speak to the Women's Branch of the British Legion at her village. Cannot agree that this would be at all nice for British Legion or for me, have never Spoken (in that sense) to anyone since long-ago days at School Debating Society. Say this, more or less, and add that I would not know what to speak *about*. Uncut Moquette simply takes this as further proof of my modest nature and says Oh AnythingWill Do, she is sure I will be Amusing and the Legion will Love It. (Reference to Beau Geste which springs instantly to mind would probably not be well received.) Before I can take firm stand and refuse absolutely, Uncut Moquette becomes very business-like, produces little notebook and says they have a Free Date in June, will that suit me? This seems so far off that I weakly agree, and she makes a note, expresses gratification, and surges away. Cannot think what came over me. Can only hope that either she or I will drop dead before June.

Distraction provided at this point by departure of Anna Farthingale, who makes Royal Progress to drawing-room door with Susan and Lady E-A in attendance as Ladies-in-Waiting, while the rest of us form respectful avenue. Am filled with wholehearted admiration for A. F. and feel that it has all been a great privilege, but bow my head as she passes not so much from reverence as from passionate desire that she should never set eyes on me again.

We all relax after limousine and chauffeur have swept her away, and show tendency to revert to normal standards of conversation (cost of living, the weather, vagaries of local post-office and well-being of our families), but Susan and Lady E-A are not having any of this and break up cosy groups of old friends and make us all go and talk to people we don't know. In general reshuffle I get headmaster of nearby prep school, towards whom I feel apologetic because rival establishment is to receive James. (This is quite illogical, must really suppress maternal conviction that all prep schools are vying with one another for privilege of educating my sons.)

Headmaster is in jovial mood, and tells me horrifying story about immoral goings-on at school belonging to acquaintance of his, where Head Prefect seduced the Matron. Am very shocked by this and say incredulously At a *Prep* School? at which he looks rather offended and says Certainly, Why not? Most of his boys are Capable before they leave. Am more shocked than ever, though sorry if I have hurt his feelings by impugning virility of his pupils, and escape from him at earliest possible opportunity.

Try to make my way back to company of Lee, who is now talking to Ruth, with feeling that I have had enough of the Great World and its shocks, but am prevented by Susan who presents me to Clever London Friends. (Had no idea Susan had such an extensive acquaintance.) Clever London Friends, vivacious couple with bright eyes, have much to say and apparently know all about everyone and everything in the Public Eye; have considerable difficulty in keeping up with their conversation which is mainly concerned with recent Exhibition of Sculpture, *tachiste* painting and erudite items on B.B.C. Third Programme. Mention of B.B.C. leads to exciting revelation that Clever Friends actually have much to do with broadcasting; feel that at last we have reached common ground, and tell them about my present state of anxiety regarding Miss Appleyard and possibility of my own broadcast. One of Clever Friends exclaims at this, Oh, old Sal Appleyard (which strikes me as *lèse majesté*), he knows her well and will probably be seeing her tomorrow. Nice girl. (Am personally withholding judgment as to Miss A's niceness or otherwise until I learn whether or not she requires me to broadcast.) Clever Friend promises to jog Old Sal's memory about me, and am grateful, though slightly indignant that the whole question is to him of very minor importance indeed. Should very much like to point out that it may be an Episode to him, but it is an Epoch to me, but this *bon mot* like so many others does not occur to me until we have parted company.

End of party now definitely in sight, head is swimming and shoes are purest agony, but am able to assure Susan truthfully in farewell that party has been thoroughly enjoyable. Very nearly add that I am astonished and impressed at high level of intelligence among her guests, but Lee with husbandly prescience evidently sees this coming and hurries me away.

Tell him on the way home about Uncut Moquette and idiotic promise to Speak to British Legion in June, and he is much amused and suggests that She must have thought I was Someone Else. Same suspicion had crossed my own mind, but am not pleased; feelings undergo complete revulsion and I assure him with some heat that there is No Reason why I shouldn't give a talk as well as anyone else. (Can think of many reasons, actually, and am annoyed at having committed myself, but can see no way out now, and can only make cowardly decision not to give the matter another thought till May at the very earliest.)

Wake up several times during what remains of the night in order to rehearse various versions of subject and content of Talk.

*Sunday, 18th*
Owing to persistent but misguided notion that today is a Day of Rest, breakfast is belated and leisurely. Sole result of this, as far as I am concerned, is to reduce Day of Rest into frenzied gallop to get house tidy, get lunch prepared and get ready for Church, all of which has not surprising effect of causing me to become cross and unpopular. Depart eventually to Church with strong conviction that everyone is thankful to be rid of me.

Lee spends entire day battling with wallpaper and Caves of Lascaux. Am impressed and delighted to find that popular ideas about Father Papering the Parlour are quite outdated, as he performs prodigies of skill with Bold Stripes and dining-room begins to look unrecognisably elegant. (Hope dining-room table will in time recover from liberal application of paste, and wish that best clothes-brush was not the only thing he could find to smooth wrinkles out of paper, but feel that these are finicking female criticisms that I had better keep to myself.)

Decide at lunch-time that customary trend of conversationWill Not Do, if we want our children to grow up intelligent conversationalists (Sit up Properly, Don't kick, Leave Ben Alone, Don't Talk with Your Mouth Full, Keep your Elbows to Yourself); suggest accordingly that we should institute system of General Knowledge Questions. Children are enthusiastic about this, and immediately ask several questions with their mouths full, all about Space. James goes so far as to deliver short lecture about distance of Saturn from the moon, and spills his glass of water whilst showing us exactly what he means. Mop him up and beg him to be quiet a minute, as Daddy is going to be Question Master.

Lee very cleverly plays for time by asking Toby to tell him All he Knows about Nelson. Toby makes long rambling and mainly inaccurate speech (footnotes by James, also inaccurate), which gives us all time to think up questions.

These prove in the event to be varied, and reveal many interesting facts, chief of which being that we are all lamentably ignorant. Lee exhibits tendency to show off his knowledge of German literature to Greta, and defeats her with question about Works of Schiller, and she appears mortified. Spring to her instant defence by assuring her that Lee hasn't really read *much* Schiller, to which he replies indignantly that he has read it *all*, and I retort with witty intent All Schiller and Charybdis too I suppose? which makes him laugh but throws Greta into frantic flutter of earnest questionings as to Who is This Charybdis?

Children fortunately interrupt at this stage imploring further questions, and try them out accordingly on

Literature. Who wrote *Charge of the Light Brigade*? After much thought James suggests Shakespeare, and Toby automatically says Nelson. No no no, I say, *think*, I know you read it at school, it's by Somebody Lord Something. They ponder deeply and we all wait with breathless attention until at last James' brow clears and he says It Must have been Lord Effingham. Toby corrects him briskly and says No it wasn't it was Lord Nelson. Incipient fight is suppressed by Lee who tells them It was Tennyson, both boys say they have never *heard* of Tennyson, and by mutual consent we abandon high academic plane and revert to old friends Tables.

Could wish that my own standards in this direction were a little higher, have to perform considerable feats of counting on my fingers as unobstrusively as possible when James attacks me with Nine Times Table, but all is wasted as I do not recite it according to the liturgical form apparently dictated by Miss Young, and James and Toby are united in reproving me when I say, in ordinary conversational tones, Nine Threes are Thirty-six. Not only am I wrong (which I must crossly admit, after thought), but I *should* say, as they proceed to demonstrate to me in chanting chorus, Three Nines are *Twenty*-seven, Four Nines are *Thirty*-six, Five nines are . . . interrupt them ruthlessly at this point as I do not admire tune or execution of chant, and feel in my old-fashioned way that tables recited back-to-front like this are quite unnatural. (Cannot keep up with Modern Methods of Education at all, Look-and-Say gave me equal trouble. Had better make my mind up to it, once and for all, that I am a Back Number.)

Psalm-like chant of Nine Times Table however remains rooted ineradicably in my brain for rest of day.

Mrs Parnell appears over fence during afternoon while I am searching for windfalls in orchard, and hails me with habitual air of melancholy. She hears that James is to go away to school, unnatural she calls it, him such a baby. Say bracingly that It will be Good for him, and she shakes her head at my maternal callousness and asks Why I have children if I'm not going to Enjoy them? All this Talk about Education, she continues dismissingly, Its a Mother's Love they need, and what's wrong with the village school Anyway? Know all too well that whatever I reply she will continue to think me both heartless and snobbish, and anyway she gives me no chance to justify myself as she proceeds to make further offensive suggestion that She supposes it'll make things easier for me to have him Off my Hands? Say indignantly that On the contrary, I shall miss him very much, but she ignores this and says It'll be lonely for poor little Toby won't it? He'd better come round and play with Jennie sometimes, he could always have a ride on the pony and watch the Telly. Very kind of her, am most grateful, though cannot but reflect that we should never be able to return hospitality on equally magnificent scale; make vague grateful murmurs and endeavour to bring conversation to an end by saying Well I've got a lot to do, but she sweeps this aside and tells me all about recent appearance on Television of Housewife, who, she asserts, made her think of me. Cannot think why, as it transpires that Housewife was mother of six, ran a guest-house unaided, had written two books and bought a caravan with the proceeds. Am astonished and impressed, and Mrs P goes on to tell me that Housewife had wonderful figure, was very pretty, and had assured viewers that there was Never a Cross Word in her family. Cannot resist asking why Mrs P was reminded of me? Oh, she says sadly, it wasn't that she *reminded* her of me, it was just that she made her *think* of me. Quite see that there is all the difference, and feel unfairly prejudiced against paragon of a Housewife. (Do not understand why my own labours, which are evidently as nothing compared with those of others, should invariably make me feel overworked and ill-used; can only suppose answer lies in my own natural incompetence. Bad choice dear Lee made.)

At this point Mrs P evidently notices that I have become properly abject, and cheers up quite noticeably. Ah well, she says in conclusion, No Doubt it's All for the Best (what is?), and she must Get On as she is Turning Out the Spare Room. Say sympathetically Housework is a Perfect Nuisance, isn't it? at which she is astonished and says Oh but it Gives us Something to Do, doesn't it? Mrs P's views on desirable occupations to pass the time evidently so widely divergent from mine as to make further conversation hopeless, can only agree, with complete lack of truthfulness, and leave her to her chosen pastime.

Return to house in dejection, but am restored by discovery that Lee has practically finished dining-room, and Bold Stripes are definitely successful; we all congratulate him warmly, and agree that room is reminiscent of advertisement in favourite Glossy Magazine. James says that All it needs now is a Black Fitted Carpet; am impressed with his artistic vision and only wish we could afford it. J becomes quite wrapped up in his picture of Ideal Room and elaborates theme with eloquence; very low chairs, triangular table, and then Daddy could take a photograph of the room with a Blonde in it. Am startled by introduction of Blonde, and ask Whether I would do? James is scornful and says crushingly You're not a Blonde. Say spiritedly Yes I am, anyone with Fair Hair is a Blonde, he's one himself if it comes to that. James is pitying about my *naïveté* and says That's not what *he* means by a Blonde. Do not like to ask what he *does* mean, but make inner resolve to wean him away from Comic Strips and Glossy Magazines at an early opportunity; feel that strict diet of Henty and Arthur Ransome is indicated.

Toby breaks long reverie at this stage in order to bang table with the flat of his hand like an angry Chairman calling us to order, and says with passionately blazing blue eyes that The Point Is, God Died to Save us All.

Family conversation, indeed maternity in all its aspects, is quite definitely beyond me.

*Monday, 19th*

Post, usually so boring, suddenly goes mad and brings high drama in all directions. Lee receives communication telling him of possible new job for him in Scotland, B.B.C. breaks inscrutable silence and writes that it *will* require me to do broadcast, and complimentary copy arrives of small magazine to which I have contributed frivolous article.

Date of broadcast is distant, have unreasonable inner conviction that it will prove to be thoroughly inconvenient

201

(shall probably find ourselves in Scotland by then); but am, naturally, delighted by prospect. Re-read Miss Appleyard's letter several times and feel definitely swollen-headed; this reaction intensified when I turn to magazine and scrutinise own article. Read this with passionate attention and am downcast; not only is article not as screamingly funny as I supposed when I wrote it, but it is quite distinctly bad and amateurish in places. Decide to read it all over again, pretending I am detached reader, to see how it would have struck me if I hadn't written it . . . but am interrupted at this stage by Lee who wishes to tell me more about Scotland.

We all have much to say about Scotland.

James and Toby point excitedly to brawny kilted figure on packet of porridge oats and say That's what Scotsmen look like, and Please can they have kilts, and Do Scotsmen talk English?

I say with considerable restraint that I suppose this is going to mean Yet Another Move, and that as this is the eleventh in ten years we ought to be getting used to it by now, and does Lee want to take his Oars?

Lee begs us all to restrain ourselves and says repressively that the whole thing is Only Tentative and may yet Not Come Off. (Nonetheless, am prepared to bet it will, if only because he has just taken all that trouble papering dining-room.)

Amidst general excitement had rather forgotten about Greta, but am sharply reminded of her now as I suddenly observe that she is weeping bitterly, and Toby is gazing at her in something regrettably nearer to amusement than sympathy. Send him and James away to get ready for school and give her belated attention. (Can she be distressed at prospect of Scotland? or was Toby kicking her? or have I been overworking her? Probably all three.) Am on the whole relieved to notice that she is clutching letter from Germany and that it, rather than our ill-usage, is evident cause of grief.

Very difficult to get any information out of her at all, but at length amidst tumultuous sobs she utters to the effect that it is her Fiancé, he is Operate. Oh dear, how sorry I am, I say; I hope he is getting better now? Amid renewed wails Greta says Ach yes but he is Operate and he is Not Tell Her. It is his Ulcus and perhaps he Die and he is Not Tell Her. Administer as much sympathy as I can, and try to reassure her that he will not die and that he only didn't tell her to save her from worrying . . . but she does not at all wish to be comforted and rushes away to her room weeping harder than ever. Am really very sorry for her but have no idea what to do about it for the present, can only leave her to orgy of grief for the time being, and resolve to have calm soothing session with her later.

For the time being am fully occupied getting Lee and boys out of house and removing Ben from larder where he is quietly eating stale cheese.

Lee's parting words are that I'm not to start working up a Great Thing about Scotland as it will probably never come to anything. Promise that I won't, but find myself, as soon as he is out of sight, giving much thought to problems of Moving House, Scottish Schools for Toby and Ben, and What about More Blankets as it will be Cold Up There?

Interrupted by front door bell. (Pray that it is not the decayed gentlewoman who has tendency to arrive at this hour to tell me that I don't read the Bible.) It is not, on the contrary, it is earnest hairy young man in sandals, clasping

sheaf of foolscap notes, conducting Poll. Welcome him warmly, at which he seems astonished, but in fact have always longed to be in on a Poll and am quite prepared to spend entire morning telling him every single thing about my life.

Hairy Young Man doesn't want to know every single thing about my life, snubbingly refuses my hospitable invitation to Come in and Sit Down, but simply asks How do we Heat our Water? Very disappointed, had hoped for something far more dramatic in the way of interview. However, make as much as I can of boiler and its eccentricities, and am just getting quite lyrical about how well it goes when it *does* go, when young man cuts me short and asks Who looks after it? Do I have a Man? Reply flippantly that I have a Husband, if that counts? but young man is not amused and simply continues with *questionnaire*. Does he *like* doing the boiler? (Can only reflect that this is the silliest question I ever heard in my life, how could anyone *like* doing a *boiler*?) Do not, however, like to be too emphatic in my description of the way in which malevolent spirit of the boiler dominates our days, from foolish super-stitious conviction that if I say too much boiler will hear me, and Go Out. Modify my reply accordingly, which entails many circumlocutions and half-truths (Well he doesn't exactly *like* it, but he doesn't actually *mind*); young man makes very brief note on foolscap at this stage, have horrid fear that he has put me down as Seventy-five per cent Don't Know.

See him off (hope he will get on well with Mrs Parnell), and go back and give boiler a little extra placatory helping of coke just in case it *did* hear.

Rest of day, which I should like to spend gloating over B.B.C. and magazine article, has in fact to be spent coping with Greta, whose grief continues unrestrainedly. Try every encouraging reaction I can think of, from bracing optimism to positively morbid sympathy, but all to no avail, she goes on sobbing hysterically and reiterating that He is Operate and He Has not Tell Her, and Never More can she Trust Him, and What shall she do? Ask eventually if she would like to go back to Germany? At this she weeps afresh, but I think looks faintly brighter. Tell her not to decide now, but to think about it, and let me know later if she *does* wish to go.

By the evening she has recovered sufficiently to make up her mind that she *does* wish to go back to Germany. We are soothing and say Yes of course, we will arrange it, and tell her that we shall Miss Her Very Much. At this she looks tearful again and tells us that Never Never will she Forget us, this sweet Bennie, she is so sorry not to stay but it is her Fiancé, he is Operate . . . cut her short as kindly as possible at this stage as I do not think I can listen to familiar saga even once more; and she retires to bed looking wan but I think calmer.

Decide to Do Out Kitchen Cupboards in view of possible move to Scotland, and Lee brings in shoe-cleaning equipment in order to keep me company. He also brings magazine and reads my article with profound attention, and is nice about it, going so far as to assert that What with this and the Broadcast I have really Got Going, and What about this book I am supposed to be writing? Won't that publisher be waiting?

Toy pleasingly for a while with vision of Demon King pacing his office, biting his nails, work at a standstill until my masterpiece arrives . . . but abandon it to point out that I have one or two other matters to attend to first.

What are they? asks Lee sceptically.

Well, there's this School Concert. I can't concentrate on much until that's over. And if Greta is really going back to Germany there is that to think about and once she has gone I shall be tied to the house again.

All the better for Writing, says Lee unsympathetically;

so far he doesn't see the difficulty, what else have I got to do?

Point out that there is This Play with Lady E-A, and that not only do we have to go to several more rehearsals but we shall now have to find baby-sitters for the actual performances. And he will have to Learn his Part into the bargain, I add, feeling that it is time for me to do some attacking.

He begs me to mind my own business, and tell him what else prevents me from writing day and night.

Rack my brains and then, with astonishment that I should ever have forgotten it, recall Broadcast. Cannot possibly concentrate on anything until that is over.

Lee still unconvinced, but I think shows slight symptoms of agreement when I add that there is also the prospect of Getting James ready for his Prep School, buying uniform, dealing with Cash's names and tuckboxes and other as yet unfamiliar accoutrements. (Can well foresee that in the years ahead these will become all too familiar.)

By this stage am convinced that I am never going to have time to write another letter, let alone book, and when I add that I thought he wanted us to Give a Party Too even Lee admits that life begins to look crowded, and asks whether I think that perhaps that had better wait until after Christmas, if we aren't in Scotland by then?

*Christmas!*

Had forgotten all about Christmas.

Totally unchristian reaction at this reminder is unadulterated horror. (Sometimes think that the roles of housewife and practising Christian are quite incompatible.) Remember that we have not dealt with presents for Lee's parents in

New Zealand, that we must order turkey and quantities of expensive food, that I must make Christmas cake and puddings, and deal with cards and presents. Grandpapa will want to know what to give the boys, the boys will want to know what to give Grandpapa and Lee and each other, I shall have to give everybody something and I haven't any money, and Great-Aunt Elizabeth in particular will deserve something really spectacular this year.

Lee interrupts my agitated harangue at this stage to say that This year he proposes to Make most of his presents, a decision which apparently fills him with contentment, but which pleases me less as I have conviction that it simply means he will do nothing at all until Christmas Eve when he will suddenly dash out to do conscience-stricken shopping.

Also realise that if Greta is no longer with us we shall have the spare room free and can have Grandpapa to stay, which will be splendid but will entail further efforts at Gracious Living as he does not consider scrambled eggs an adequate supper and will, not unreasonably, expect adequate supply of bathwater in addition to four square meals a day in the dining-room, not to mention fairly frequent respites from the company of his grandsons. (Wonder if we could temporarily convert the attic into sound-proof playroom?)

*Tuesday 20th*
Resolve to deal with everything in calm collected fashion. Cannot escape conviction that I should be better able to do this if normal life did not have to continue simultaneously

with packing, Greta and her departure plans, and elaborate organisation apparently inseparable from Christmas.

Find, as the day wears on, that far from being calm and collected I am spending all my time standing about evolving fifty-three highly complicated and irreconcilable Master Plans and achieving absolutely nothing. Wonder if this state indicates incipient Nervous Breakdown? How nice, if so; then someone else could take over everything while I had a peaceful rest in a Home. Family cares as usual, however, assert themselves at this point and I abandon profitless mental meanderings and tidy sitting-room, which looks like a stall at a Jumble Sale. Conglomeration on writing-desk reveals forgotten letter from old School-friend, which asked so trenchantly What I was doing with My Brain these days?

Any possible truthful answer to this query so obviously unsatisfactory that I can only resolve to shelve the entire question until the children are grown-up, when Brain, such as it is, may perhaps come out of retirement.

Meanwhile, shall make no further attempt to justify myself or my education to anyone, and concentrate on Being Practical.

End of Diary.

*Also available from Virago Modern Classics*

## THE DIARY OF A PROVINCIAL LADY
### E. M. Delafield

The Provincial Lady has a nice house, a nice husband (usually asleep behind *The Times*) and nice children. In fact, maintaining niceness is the Provincial Lady's goal in life – her *raison d'etre*. She never raises her voice, rarely ventures outside Devon (why would she?), only occasionally allows herself to become vexed by the ongoing servant problem, and would be truly appalled by the confessional mode of the late twentieth century. The Provincial Lady is, after all, part of what made Britain great.

Also published here are the three enchanting sequels to *The Diary of a Provincial Lady*: *The Provincial Lady Goes Further*, *The Provincial Lady in America* and *The Provincial Lady in Wartime*.

**'I re-read, for the nth time, E. M. Delafield's dry, caustic *Diary of a Provincial Lady*, and howled with laughter' – *India Knight***

# LOVE LESSONS

*Joan Wyndham*

August 1939. As a teenage catholic virgin, Joan Wyndham spent her days in London's bohemian Chelsea trying to remain pure and her nights trying to stay alive. Huddled in the air-raid shelter, she wrote secretly and obsessively in her diary about the strange yet exhilarating times she was living through, sure that this was 'the happiest time of my life'.

*Monday, 13th May 1940 – After Jo had gone I looked at my flushed face in the glass and I tidied my hair, thinking what an awful tart I am. There was a terrible love-bite on my neck, so I got a pin and made a few scratches across it and told Mummy a cat had scratched me, but I don't think she believed me. Later we listened to a very stirring speech by Churchill about 'blood, toil, sweat and tears.'*

**'A latter-day Pepys in camiknickers'** – *Scotland on Sunday*

# TIME AFTER TIME

*Molly Keane*

The Swifts – three sisters of marked eccentricity, defiantly christened April, May and baby June, and their only brother, one-eyed Jasper – have little in common, save vivid memories of their darling mother and a long lost youth particularly prone to acts of treachery.

Into their world comes cousin Leda from Vienna, a visitor from the past, blind but beguiling, a thrilling guest. Within days, the lifestyle of the Swifts has been dramatically overturned – and desires, dormant for so long, flame fierce and bright like never before.

**'Sharp, deadly and irresistibly funny'** – *Daily Telegraph*

## Now you can order superb titles directly from Virago

| | | | |
|---|---|---|---|
| ☐ | The Diary of a Provincial Lady | E. M. Delafield | £8.99 |
| ☐ | Love Lessons | Joan Wyndham | £7.99 |
| ☐ | Time After Time | Molly Keane | £6.99 |

Please allow for postage and packing: **Free UK delivery.**
Europe; add 25% of retail price; Rest of World; 45% of retail price.

To order any of the above or any other Virago titles, please call our credit card orderline or fill in this coupon and send/fax it to:

**Virago, P.O. Box 121, Kettering, Northants NN14 4ZQ**
**Tel: 01832 737526   Fax: 01832 733076**
**Email: aspenhouse@FSBDial.co.uk**

☐ I enclose a UK bank cheque made payable to Virago for £ ............

☐ Please charge £.............. to my Access, Visa, Delta, Switch Card No.

☐☐☐☐☐☐☐☐☐☐☐☐☐☐☐☐☐☐☐

Expiry Date ☐☐☐☐   Switch Issue No. ☐☐

NAME (Block letters please) ...................................................................

ADDRESS ..............................................................................................

...............................................................................................................

...............................................................................................................

Postcode ..................................Telephone ...............................................

Signature ...............................................................................................

Please allow 28 days for delivery within the UK. Offer subject to price and availability.

Please do not send any further mailings from companies carefully selected by Virago ☐